# SEXY LIAR

### Dirty Hacker #1

*A Dirty Little Secret Duet*

USA TODAY BESTSELLING AUTHOR

## STACEY KENNEDY

Print Edition

Stacey Kennedy
www.staceykennedy.com

Edited by Christa Soulé Désir
Proofed by Trisha Tobias
Cover Photograph: iStock
Cover Design by Sweety 'n Spicy Designs

Manufactured in Canada

First Edition August 2019

*For all the readers who hoped Alex*
*would get her story!*

# PROLOGUE

THE FLASHES OF red and blue filled the dark sky as CIA Agent Rowan Hawke watched the Paris police handcuff Roger Moore, a hired hitman who'd evaded the CIA for months and had been on the FBI's Most Wanted List for years.

"A job well done, Hawke," the seductive voice hummed in his ear through his earpiece.

Alex McCoy. The best hacker in San Francisco. As a teenager, she was arrested for hacking into the CIA databases, and then she quietly got released under the agreement that she'd do contract work when her government—both the CIA and the FBI—needed her. When she's not being ordered around by the Feds, she works in San Francisco for Blackwood Security, a private security detail company.

She'd come onto the case a week ago, and the magic had been there between them since after their first meeting when they ended up screwing in the basement parking lot of the Paris PD headquarters.

"You're being too kind," Rowan said, turning away

from the scene and striding down the thin, dark alley with the cobblestone roads. "You're the one who found him. I just chased him down."

Alex's laughter brushed across his scenes. "Well, that's true, but you did all the running. Much, much harder."

She never spoke with the arrogance she was due. Her mind was sharp and quick, and Rowan had been impressed by her from the second he met her. Which only continued when she put her hands on his body. Rowan had prided himself on being able to walk away from any woman. He needed to as part of his job description. Only this time, his feet moved him in the wrong direction.

When he didn't fill the silence, she said, "I guess this is goodbye, then."

"I guess it is," he replied.

The case was done. Rowan planned on leaving Alex right after Moore was in custody and returning to New York City to await his next case. But he needed one more of taste of her. One more feel of her.

Rowan finally reached the place where the CIA had put them up. He entered the Hôtel Fleur, a boutique hotel set right in the heart of the city, and trotted up the stairs until he used his keycard to open the door. The room held Paris elegance with flowered wallpaper, antique furniture, and old paintings of people in

Victorian times. Luxurious grand curtains were on either side of the only window in the room with the metal balcony. What interested Rowan more was the woman standing at that window.

Alex's bright amber eyes locked onto him, her dark hair draping over her shoulder. "You said you were leaving."

"I did," he told her, shutting the door then closing the distance between them.

She tilted her head back and stared at his lips, nibbling her own, emotion flaring in her eyes. "Then why are you here?"

He shouldn't be, but Rowan couldn't help himself. He slid his hands across her face, loving the color that rose to her cheeks and how her mouth parted, then he threaded his fingers into her hair. "That's a very good question." With his other hand, he tucked a finger in the front of her jeans and tugged her to him. Her pupils dilated and her breath grew raspy. When he touched her, she melted, and damn, was it a rush. He opened her jeans and yanked her pants and panties down.

The heat in her gaze bore into his when she opened his jeans. "Should we talk about why you came back?"

He kicked off his pants and slid his hands down to her bottom as she stepped out of her jeans. "Yeah, we should definitely talk about that." But he wouldn't talk about it. He didn't ever talk about these things. He took his pleasures. That's where things stopped for him.

Only this time, he wanted one more taste before he walked away.

He sealed his mouth against hers, kissing her with all the intensity burning through him, and she moaned against his mouth. Urgency had him deepening the kiss, roughly holding her, imprinting this memory into his mind. He slowly walked her back until she was up against the wall. Not wasting any time, he grabbed a condom from the box they had on the end table and sheathed himself. When he looked her way again, Alex was primed and ready up against the wall. Her cheeks were flushed, eyes dark with need. He returned to her, hooked her leg onto his arm and entered her, while he fisted his other hand into her hair.

This time, he didn't kiss her. No, he stared at her intimately. And she watched him right back.

She was tight, wet, and perfect with every slow stroke he gave, warming them both up. He'd learned the ways of her lithe body. Her breath was steady, lips parted slightly. "Not enough, luv?"

Her eyes twinkled.

He thrust forward. Hard.

Those eyes went huge and she smiled. "Better."

He kept at that rhythm. Slow, but hard, until he caught the desperation in her eyes. Only then did he pick up speed, taking them both where they wanted to go.

Over the edge. Together.

And when they did break apart, it was rough, loud, and she clung to him, more than she ever had before.

But then he forced her to let go, knowing if he didn't, he wasn't sure he would. She'd gotten a hold of him in ways no one had before her. When he caught her gaze, he saw that same conflict on her face too.

"Just give me a minute before we talk, okay?" she asked softly.

He released her leg and stepped back. "Of course."

Silently, she gathered her clothes and headed for the bathroom. Rowan dressed back in his jeans and then stared at the closed bathroom door. He couldn't stay. He *never* stayed. Hearing the sink's faucet turn on, he headed for the door, knowing he'd always planned to leave the very first time he placed his lips on hers.

# CHAPTER 1

*Five years later…*

O N THE CRISP autumn night in the heart of Manhattan, Rowan had a new assignment: Secure his target—former lover, Alex McCoy—to help catch New York City's latest serial killer, recently coined by the media the Casanova Sadist. Of all the assignments he'd taken since the last time he saw her, this one filled him with the most dread.

When he arrived at the Cool Cat's Piano Bar in New York City's Theater District a little after nine o'clock at night, he noted how the jet-black walls, the cushy booths, and crystal chandeliers set the mood of older, classier times. Alex sat at the bar, drinking a martini. Her long dark hair flowed down her back over her black leather jacket, her tight ass in her blue jeans drawing his attention. He'd remembered that body, every spectacular inch of her.

He never expected to work with her again. Let alone see her again.

Five years had gone by since they had spent that

week together in Paris. Five years since he'd smelled the captivating spring-like scent that belonged only to her. An aroma that had a slight similarity to when the sun came out after it rained. Five years since she set those gorgeous intelligent amber eyes of hers on him. Five years since the unexplainable passion burning between them made him hard in a single breath. And five years since he'd told himself not to go to San Francisco to apologize for running out on her, when he very well knew she'd begun to care for him. Alex had been his biggest regret. The only woman he thought about after he left her. Maybe because she'd had a hold on him too.

He moved closer, the chatter from the busy bar brushing over him. While Alex still worked for Blackwood Security in San Francisco, she'd come to New York City for a vacation, which put her on his radar. He learned through the CIA's undercover New York location where he'd been earlier today that she'd landed at John F. Kennedy International Airport. Alex was one of the best hackers out there. When she moved, the CIA kept a close eye on her, and her arriving in New York City set off alarms throughout the CIA. But the second he heard she was in town, he knew she could help him crack this case.

Only problem?

He'd run out on her without a word.

The man at the piano on stage played a soft, sensual

song, setting the right mood for what exactly Rowan needed to do. He could manipulate easily. That was his job, and he needed to get her back on his side before asking for her help. Alex was smart. He knew he needed to tread lightly when he slid on the stool next to her. "Whiskey on the rocks," he said to the bartender.

He noted the hitch of Alex's breath before he caught the surprise in her wide eyes, which she controlled in an instant. Her gaze lingered on his mouth long enough to let him know she hadn't forgotten him—or the sensual pull they shared—either. A bonus for him, making this seduction easier.

"You know I don't believe in coincidences," she finally said.

Rowan didn't either. He also didn't believe in lasting love. He trusted no one, and most times people around him got killed, which didn't lend itself well to long-term relationships. But lust was real, and that red-hot sexual energy still pulsed between him and Alex, almost so tangible he could taste it in the air. "Yes, I do know that about you."

She didn't even miss a beat, glancing down at her drink in her hands. "How did you know I was here?"

"Your arrival at JFK raised alarms."

Alex snorted. "Are you here to check up on me, then?"

The bartender placed his drink down in front of him.

He nodded his thanks and left a ten-dollar bill on the bar then lifted his glass to Alex. "I can certainly think of better things to do than check up on you, can't you?"

Instant heat flared in her eyes in the same way it had five years ago. Rowan wanted desperately to drink it in. And that had nothing to do with the reasons that brought him there tonight.

But that heat also made his job easier. He'd play on that desire, getting her to reconnect and forget that he'd left her once. She had no reason to help him. Christ, she had no reason to talk to him. He had to give her one. So he'd come up with a plan: seduce her, earn her for-giveness, find the killer.

Rowan lifted his glass. "To old times."

She clinked his glass with a sexy smile. "To old times."

They hadn't stayed for a second drink.

An Uber ride later, and with heat burning in the air between them, Rowan followed Alex through the hallway of Langdon Bridge, the swankiest hotel in New York City where Alex had checked into. "Nice place," he said, entering the room after her.

She shut the door behind him and then locked it. "I'm supposed to be pampering myself on vacation."

He couldn't help himself, and a grin tugged on his mouth. "I promise you'll be pampered tonight, McCoy."

She returned the grin, though her smile dripped with

lust. "Classy, Hawke."

"Always." He took in the lavish modern suite, finding they stood in a small living room, while she strode by him and dropped the key card on the table by the door. The bedroom was in the next room with double doors and a large king-size bed with a white duvet. Obviously, her boss paid her well, as he should. Good—*honest*—hackers were hard to find. Rowan began to glance over at her, when he caught sight of her laptop sitting on the coffee table near the large row of windows by the wingback chairs. A laptop that he knew she could do things with that nearly no one else could do. There was no place that Alex could not get into. No person she could not find.

That's why he needed her. He sought answers about the Casanova Sadist that no one had been able to give him. A killer that he'd been hunting for weeks now. A killer that had taken the lives of five women, leaving their naked bodies bound and displayed like they were a disturbing piece of art. A killer that still had three more women in his grips.

But first, he needed Alex on his side. He needed for her to *want* to help him, instead of flipping him off and telling him to find someone else. Which was exactly what he deserved.

Determined to reconnect and put his plan into action, he yanked her lithe body up against his and ravished her with his mouth, pleased when she kissed him back with equal fervor.

But soon that wasn't enough. He needed…*more.*

With every bit of clothing he removed from her body, he knew the deeper he was getting himself in this. Touching her reminded him of the exact reasons he'd run. She felt too good…too real…too dangerous. But there was no turning back now, not with lives on the line.

He lived his life in the shadows. He'd spent so much time pretending to be other people to catch criminals, he couldn't even remember the man he was meant to be. Until Alex. And that rich sensation of *home* that she pulled out of him would not wait. He wanted her. Every goddamn perfect inch of her.

With each kiss, her mouth molded to his. Her body bent to his will, reacting to every one of his touches, urging him on like a drug he couldn't get enough of. He wanted her like he hadn't wanted anything for a long time. She tasted sweet and yet sinful, and he ached to drink her in. Every brush of her lips, swirl of her tongue, only made him thirstier. She held his T-shirt tight, yanking him closer, until she removed his shirt and then pushed him away a moment with a gasp.

He met her lust-filled eyes, and his cock pressed painfully against the zipper of his jeans. "Still so dangerously sexy, I see," he told her huskily.

She licked her lips. "Likewise, Hawke."

His muscles felt rigid beneath his skin as he scanned over her creamy flesh to her black lace bra covering a perfect handful of breasts.

"Don't get any ideas about this," she said, drawing his focus back to her face. She kicked off her red high heels. "We've got tonight, then you forget me again."

That seemed to be their thing. When someone saw the darkness that lurked beneath people's skin, that's all they saw. Trust came hard after that. "I'll take tonight." He stalked toward her. His target. "But you won't get any agreement from me that I won't want more or that I'll forget you."

When he reached her, he grasped her hip. She gasped when he yanked her against him, her face flushing beautifully. He pinned her arms behind her, dropping his head into her neck, inhaling the sweetness of her flowery perfume. He kissed at her flesh roughly, encouraged by the unleashed moan she gave. Hot and hard and ready to give them both a release, he backed her up against the wall. She draped her leg across his thigh, and he took that as an invitation. He ground his throbbing cock against the junction between her thighs, moving his mouth to hers again. Then he devoured her.

Every moan, he drank in.

Each one of her shivers, he owned.

Desperate to have her, he leaned away to drag his

fingers over the curve of her breasts and damn near salivated. "Exquisite," he murmured.

"No, Hawke," she said, and he lifted his gaze up to her smoldering eyes as she took his hand and placed it between her thighs. "In case you forgot, here is where I'm really exquisite."

He felt her heat through the denim, and he grinned at the challenge, not minding a little power play between them. He could always give the illusion of control, knowing in the end, he'd always get it back. He flicked the button of her jeans open then yanked them down to below her ass. With his free hand, he slid his fingers into the soft strands of her hair, until he held her tight, right where he wanted her. When he fisted his fingers, her hooded eyes met his. Only then did he slide his other hand into the front of her panties. He met trimmed pubic hair and a soaking wet sex. "I've never forgotten, Alex. Not a single thing." Her taste, her smell, how beautiful she looked when she fell apart, all of it had remained cemented in his mind. He stroked the silkiness of her folds, bringing her arousal to her clit where he circled the bud.

She moaned, her eyes fluttering, as she dropped her head back against the wall. "Don't stop."

He leaned in, bringing his mouth close to hers, tasting the passion in the air between them. "Tell me what you want," he ordered, nipping at her jawline.

She opened her rich, seductive eyes. "Make me come, Rowan."

His muscles quivered at his name on her tongue. A tongue he wanted back in his mouth and then later on his cock. But it was the heady lust in the single word that drove him to give her what she wanted. He easily inserted one finger into her drenched heat and then another.

Her eyes fluttered. "Fuck yes…"

Captivated by how sensual and free she was, he tightened his fingers in her hair, seeing the swell of desire rushing across her face. Needing to get his cock where his fingers were, he didn't drag this out. He settled his fingers in deep, played with a few different moves to learn her tells again, and then he quickly found his rhythm. He thrust his fingers fast and hard, working her pleasure until he had full control of her body.

Then he went even harder.

It didn't take long for her to break apart around him after that. Her breath hitched, muscles tightened, and her expression pinched. For a single moment in time, she hung, suspended on the highest peak of pleasure before she screamed his name and shuddered, coming beautifully against his fingers until the only thing helping her stand was his hand in her hair and his fingers deep in her quivering sex.

Lost in her all the same, he gave her the minute she

needed to recover.

When she finally reopened her eyes, giving him a sexy smile, he withdrew his hand from her panties.

"Your turn." She pressed against his chest, sending him walking backward until she had him in the bedroom. When his legs met the bed, he sat, and she pushed harder until he was lying down. "But first, I've got a surprise for you."

"I don't need a surprise." He leaned up on one arm. "I want you." Her cheeks flushed pink and her mouth parted. He remembered how much he liked that turned-on look on her. "Get over here."

Her smile was pure temptation. "You'll like the surprise. Promise." She turned away before he could object again.

He glanced down at his painfully hard erection pressing against the zipper of his jeans while she retreated to the bathroom just off to the right. He anticipated the wet tightness of her sex, hearing those moans she gave get louder.

When the bathroom door finally clicked open again, he found her looking like an succubus in her black lingerie for all the control she wielded over him. He would have given her anything right then as long as she let him have her. She leaned against the doorframe and gave him a devilish smile. "So, Rowan, I've got a question for you."

"Anything, luv."

She stepped away from the door, and suddenly, he was staring down the barrel of the gun as she said, "What do you want from me?"

And just like that, he realized—more than a little annoyingly—he'd been expertly played. Not only was she smart enough to know he had a motive for sitting next to her in the bar, but she was smart enough to get an orgasm out of him before she called him out. "You don't want to do this," he warned.

She smiled again. This time, her smile was deadly.

In that very second, he lurched forward, and in the same moment, he watched her finger squeeze the trigger.

# CHAPTER 2

W*ELL, SHIT.*
Three days ago, Alex left behind her routine life in San Francisco and her boss, Ryder Blackwood, who owned Blackwood Security, one of the top private security detail companies in North America, for a well-deserved vacation. Ryder had operatives working all over the world for top government officials, diplomats, and celebrities, but Alex did all the dirty hacking back at headquarters. She worked very much in the gray space between the law. Sure, she loved running down clues, hacking into systems no one else could get into, and helping Ryder make the world a better place, but watching him get married last year reminded her that she had no personal life. All she did was work or sleep. Both the CIA and the FBI owned her. Her job owned her. There had to be more to life than working all the time, but after Lena, her younger sister, died when they were teenagers, Alex kept her nose stuck in her laptop. A therapist likely would have told her she was avoiding her emotions by keeping herself busy, but she never went to

a therapist. And she didn't want to deal with that pain.

Still, a lot of time had gone by since Lena passed away. While she missed her sister, it didn't consume her every waking minute any longer. And as she healed more every day, Alex realized she was lacking a personal life. She needed to find that happiness she felt as a new hacker, the excitement that brought a serious high. Lately, everything just felt dull. She was bored out of her mind.

Truth was, excelling at her job had some serious drawbacks, including having everyone always want something from her. *Always.* Her vacation was supposed to be her time to figure out next steps for her life.

That's precisely why after the last case she worked alongside Ryder involving a celebrity and a sex tape, Alex requested some time off. She landed in JFK airport, met one of Ryder's team members, who gave her what Ryder called a *survival kit* to keep her safe when she was in New York City, which included weapons, rope, handcuffs, throwaway phones, and laptops. That *kit* only confirmed she needed to be a normal person for a while, whatever that even was.

She'd come to New York City for the Broadway shows, for Times Square, and for the New York-style pizza and cheesecake. The Big Apple had always been on her bucket list, and she was determined to start living life again—once she figured out how to do that—instead of sitting behind her laptop letting time whiz by. But, and this may have been the biggest *but* of her life, the very last thing she expected to find on her vacation was the man who had given her the hottest week of her life and made her feel things no man had ever made her feel.

Rowan Hawke.

A dirty-blond, scruffy-faced man of mystery.

And the *only* man that ever got close to her heart.

She never could forget how he smelled like sin and sandalwood and something even more addictive than that—lust. Rowan had enough bulk to show he worked out without being obsessive about it. And those delicious muscles were currently on full display as he sat on the chair. His head was bowed, and his legs and arms expertly bound, just as Ryder had once taught her. With each sleepy breath he drew in, his square chest covered with light soft hair lifted. Her gaze roamed down over his six-pack to his jeans. God, this man was a dream.

He was also the most dangerous man she'd ever known. Not because he was lethal and could kill in a second. The danger lay within her heart. Five years ago, she'd known if she stayed with him any longer, leaving would have been impossible. She'd grown more attached to him in a week than she had after years with Ryder. And *that* was scary as hell.

The fear was a side effect of having a deadbeat father and a drug addict mother who eventually overdosed and died, as well as the pain of losing her sister. She couldn't trust a CIA agent who lived a life full of secrets. Especially with her heart. Those seven days with Rowan made her feel weak, fragile even.

She didn't do fragile. And it took a good month to feel like herself again after she came back from Paris. Tonight, when Rowan first slid on that stool next to her, she thought this was her chance to take back the key to her heart that she'd gave him. To show herself that anything she felt that week was all due to being Paris, the city of love and romance.

Of course, until she realized his intentions weren't good.

The sudden ringing on her computer snapped her focus back to her monitor. She sat with her laptop on her lap on the comfy chair in the sitting area of the expensive hotel that was part of her indulgence on this trip. She clicked the answer button of the chat program that she'd created for Ryder that was secure and untraceable. "Hi," she said when Ryder's face appeared on the screen.

Ryder's wise, stern green eyes came as an instant relief. He was bulkier than Rowan, with muscle he gained from his time in the Army Rangers. His typical dirty-blond buzz cut was longer than he ever had it, being a little shaggy around his ears. "What's wrong?" he asked, voice firm.

Alex spun the monitor to show Rowan, still sleeping.

When she turned the screen back to face her, Ryder was frowning. "I've got a problem," she told him.

"I take it this isn't some kinky play," he said with a hint of a smile. Ryder was a Dominant. He knew all about *kinky play*. Alex did not. If anyone tried to make her submit, she'd knock their teeth out faster than they could say, *kneel for me*. All she wanted was some good old-fashioned dirty sex.

And if she were being honest with herself, she *still* wanted Rowan in a big, bad way, even now.

"Sadly, this isn't a game," she explained, feeling the heat rise in her cheeks. "I shot him with a tranquilizer." She pushed the embarrassment away, knowing she'd gotten herself into something and needed Ryder as backup in case anything went sideways. "This is Rowan Hawke. He's the CIA agent I worked with five years ago on that case in Paris." Not that she had a choice. That had been part of her plea bargain. When either the CIA or the FBI needed her hacking expertise, she'd come on board. In the past ten years, she'd worked maybe six cases for them. For free.

"I remember that case," Ryder said tightly. He was at home. The abstract painting that his wife Hadley had picked up at a local art show was hung up behind him. "Is this the guy you shacked up with there?"

Alex nodded. "The very one." She'd told Ryder all about Rowan when she got back, not willingly, of course.

Ryder had pressed her when she came home feeling like she'd left half of her heart in Paris.

Ryder studied her a moment, probably gauging her mood, which was about as bad as it could get, before he addressed her again. "All right, want to explain how he ended up shot with a tranq?"

She exhaled a long, deep breath before answering him. "Hawke showed up at a bar where I was having a drink. My arriving in New York City set off some alarms, which we already knew it would."

Ryder agreed with a nod. "Expected, yes."

"Well, that spark that started in Paris"—she cleared her throat—"let's just say it hasn't diminished. We came back here, and everything was going fine until he stared at my laptop and his expression changed. It got...I don't know...intense. I saw that look on his face in Paris. He wants something from me."

Ryder's mouth twitched. "So, instead of asking him what he wants, you shot him with a tranq?"

"Damn right I did," Alex retorted with no shame. "He's up to something. Why is he not going through normal channels to get me to work with the CIA? Something isn't right."

Ryder cocked his head, his eyebrows tightening over his intense eyes. "I'm not going to argue with you. It is...*odd*."

She gave a quick nod and then studied Rowan, not

feeling a bit bad about knocking him out cold either. Knowing he was CIA and didn't go through the right channels to speak to her only made her more suspicious. Maybe he felt burned by her. This was all some type of revenge plan when she landed in New York City.

"Can you ask around about him?" she asked, turning her attention back onto Ryder. "See if he's no longer CIA, anything like that?" Ryder had contacts in every nook and cranny in the government and law enforcement agencies.

"Yeah, I can do that," Ryder said with a firm nod. A baby began crying in the background, and Ryder's gaze flicked up, obviously wanting to go to his newborn son, Colton, and his wife. "Do you need me to send someone to you?" he asked, looking at Alex again.

One word from Alex and the room would be full of ex-military that now worked for Ryder and did things that Alex probably didn't even want to think about. "I'm okay for now," she said. "I've got him tied up good. He won't be going anywhere anytime soon. I don't..." She paused, making sure she trusted her judgment. "I don't necessarily feel threatened by him." But she wouldn't rule that out quite yet. "Let me chat with him to find out what in the hell he wants from me."

"All right." Ryder paused, considered her, and then his gaze firmed. "Do not do anything risky, Alex. Get your gun, the one with bullets, and aim it at him. If he moves when you don't ask him to, shoot him in both legs. Call an ambulance, and I'll come down there to the police station to get you. You hear me?"

Ryder took on a ton of government contract work. He also gained friends in high places. When needed, he called in favors, and he used those favors wisely. She smiled. They had such an unusual but perfect friendship. They met when she hacked his system and he'd caught her. There had been something so instant when they'd met. A bond she'd never felt with anyone. It hadn't been sexual; it had been protective, and he had always felt very brotherly toward her. Ryder was the very reason she got out of a life of living in crappy apartments and working cases that would only have landed her in jail. And he was the *only* person she trusted. "I will. Promise."

"Good," he said. "Call me once you know more. And I'll check into him on my end."

She nodded. "Now go to your sweet baby and give Hadley a hug from me."

"Will do. Be safe." Ryder's smile warmed before the screen went black. He'd been in baby mode for the past few months. While mothers nested, Ryder went into full protective mode over his wife. He shadowed her, and Hadley hated every minute of it. Alex found it all sweet and just a bit amusing to watch a big tough guy turn to mush.

Coming from a house that never resembled a home,

with two shitty parents, didn't leave much room to believe in lasting love. Ryder and Hadley had Alex questioning that a bit as of late and wondering if she was missing out on something.

A low groan caused her to lift her gaze, and she found Rowan beginning to stir. She reached for her *real* weapon from the coffee table and shut her laptop. Her legs were crossed beneath her hotel-provided robe. Her body still hummed from the incredible orgasm Rowan had given her, and that was another thing she didn't feel bad about. Hell, he ruined her vacation. That was the *least* he could do for her.

She stayed perfectly silent and still, letting him wake up. When he finally came to his senses, his narrowed gray eyes met hers. "That was rude."

"So is trying to play me." She grinned.

He closed his eyes a moment and shook his head, obviously clearing the drug from his system. It took another minute for him to look at her again. This time, he stared at her with mild amusement.

She lifted her eyebrows. "Something funny?"

"Funny?" He slowly shook his head again, then said, "I'm just trying to decide if it was brilliant that you got an orgasm before shooting me with the dart, or cold, or downright evil."

She couldn't help herself and laughed a little. "Probably a bit of all three, if we're being honest."

Beneath his arm bindings, he stretched out his fingers, clearly becoming aware that there wasn't a chance in hell he was getting out of there, unless he attacked her while he was still bound in the chair.

She shook the gun at him. "Make any move and I hurt you. That's how this works."

His gaze flicked to the weapon aimed in his direction before he looked her in the eye again. "What gave me away?"

"You didn't go through the right channels, and you looked intently at my laptop, and I *know* this is not just about sex." She kept herself sharp in case he got stupid. "You're up to something, and I want to know what it is."

"Still so fucking clever," he said, sitting up a little straighter now.

Heat flooded her at the very sight of him. Rowan was gorgeous. All muscle. Pure sex. Totally masculine. And even now, Alex felt the quivers low in her body to move to him and demand more of those incredible kisses he gave to her earlier. Sex with Rowan was better than any drug. In Paris, she never got enough. Even though his dishonesty was simply a harsh reminder that she could never trust a CIA agent, not completely, she had to fight herself from climbing right back on his lap.

Something he clearly knew since intense desire burned in his eyes, darkening the gray like a stormy sky. "You can put the gun away," he said gently. "You know I won't hurt you."

"Yeah, right," she replied with a loud snort, ignoring those eyes of his. "I make the rules here. You told me tonight that when you heard I'd come into New York, you wanted to see me. Now we both know that's a lie, so what do you want from me?"

"It's not a total lie. I definitely wanted to see you again." His mouth pinched but then relaxed with his heavy sigh. "I also need your help on a case."

She scoffed. "And you thought *this* was the way to get it?"

He regarded her for a long moment before his lips thinned. "Total transparency: I thought reconnecting with you first might get you on my side to help me with a case."

Of all the things she expected him to say, that definitely wasn't it. "You could have acted like a normal person and just asked for my help."

"I wasn't sure you'd even talk to me," he stated then shrugged. "Let alone help me. I figured if I reminded you there was a lot of good between us before I left you high and dry in Paris, then you'd be more willing to help me."

She stared at him for a full minute, her mind racing with a million different thoughts. She finally blinked. "I really hate to break it to you, but *I* left in Paris."

He frowned. "No, when you went into the bathroom, I took off."

She tried to hold it together. She did, but a burst of laughter bubbled up. "Well, when I went into the bathroom, I went out through the window."

A beat. Then his mouth twitched. "Honestly?"

She nodded. "That conversation we should have had…yeah, I didn't want to have it."

"I only agreed to that conversation because I thought you wanted to have it."

She shook her head. "I only suggested it in the first place because I thought you wouldn't fuck me again otherwise. But I don't do relationships. Let alone with a CIA agent."

Heat blazed in his eyes. "But you'll fuck me?"

A responding heat flushed through her, but she held the gun firmly aimed in his direction. "That is what we did best."

"What we *do* best," he pointed out. He glanced at his bindings. "Is this really necessary?"

"Yes," she said adamantly, lifting her gun a little higher. "Keep talking."

He frowned at her weapon and then drew in a long, deep breath before addressing her again. "I'm working the Casanova Sadist case."

The name registered. She'd seen the five murders all over the news since she'd arrived in New York City and knew more women were missing.

Rowan spoke easily, his shoulders loose and relaxed,

all indicators he was telling the truth. "This killer has been using the dating app, SiR, which connects people who are involved in the BDSM lifestyle, and is abducting women."

She studied the firmness in Rowan's gaze. While she believed what he told her was the truth, she got the feeling he wasn't telling her everything. "I take it the CIA is on the case now because the FBI has hit a dead end?"

Rowan gave a slow nod. "This killer is smart. The FBI cybercrime division has hit a wall over and over again. Every time they get close, the fucker diverts them. I need you to succeed where others have failed."

She pondered what she'd heard and tapped her fingers against the chair. The killer was real. She'd heard that a week ago another young woman had been abducted by the Casanova Sadist, which led her to believe the FBI was getting nowhere on the case. That must be why Rowan was on the case now.

"Let's say I believe what you're telling me, why didn't you go through proper channels to get me to work this case?" The CIA, as well as the FBI, had her ass. She couldn't refuse any work they sent her way, or she'd get thrown into jail. The truth of that was depressing, and maybe partly why she still had no private life. Nothing in her life could really be private.

Rowan didn't even miss a beat, his expression going stone-cold. "Because the CIA doesn't know I'm working this case."

She cocked her head, watching him very closely. "Now why exactly would one of their top agents not be on the case?"

Darkness stole over any warmth in his expression, and she recognized that emotion as he went on. "Because the last victim is my little sister, Mia, and by this killer's MO, she has only two weeks before he kills her."

Alex's breath caught and her heart twisted. She knew the pain of a missing sister intimately. And when Lena had gone missing, Alex did *everything* to find her. She stared into the warm darkness of Rowan's eyes and lowered the gun to the coffee table as Rowan pleaded, "Alex, please, will you help me?"

# CHAPTER 3

THE ROPE BURNED against Rowan's flesh, and not in a good way, while he sat bound to the chair. He gave Alex the chance to process what he told her, noting during the passing seconds the dark worry in her gaze indicated she believed him. The fact that she finally set the gun down told him she understood his reasoning. But he still reeled in the knowledge that she thought she'd left him in Paris. He wasn't sure what to make of that. It eased his guilt that he'd hurt her. Though he couldn't quite shake the tension in his chest that she didn't trust him enough five years ago to be honest with him. It bothered him more than it should.

"This killer that's all over the news has taken your sister?" she eventually asked slowly.

Rowan nodded. "Yes, he did, and the only person who is going to find her is me, and hopefully you." Nothing mattered as much Mia, an innocent who didn't deserve the brutality of the Casanova Sadist.

Alex watched him closely, tapping her fingers against the armrest. "You're in a desperate spot, then?"

"Extremely desperate," he agreed, reading between the lines of what she was getting at. "I didn't want to hurt or betray you, Alex. But there is nothing I wouldn't have done to get you on my side to help me find Mia." He paused to consider how different tonight would have gone if he'd known she'd also left him. "Time is counting down. I thought you'd hate me. I needed you to *want* to help me and thought reminding you of the good moments between us would soften you up."

Her eyebrows shot up. "Sex wouldn't have been on the table otherwise?"

He grinned with all the heat burning inside him since he put his hands on her again. "Sex most definitely would have been on the table, just after we found Mia."

"Hmmm," she said, then reached for her laptop next to her weapon.

Saving her the time, he offered, "If you log into my home computer, you'll find the FBI files on this killer there." He rambled off his IP address. "I've got all the evidence and notes in a secured folder on my database."

Her fingers began flying over the keyboard. Within minutes, she had the file up and was scanning through the documents. Rowan had no doubt she was learning all the things about this case, seeing dead end after dead end. And Rowan didn't question in the least that she spent even more time reviewing information about the last victim, Mia Hawke, his twenty-five-year-old sister.

She'd been the unexpected surprise to his parents who came seven years after him.

When Alex finally shut her laptop, she let out a long sigh and said, "Well, it looks like you're not going to die for ruining my vacation."

The crushing hopelessness that had been weighing him down lifted. "Does that mean you're agreeing to help me find my sister?"

She cocked her head to examine him, and Rowan saw the hesitation on her face. She now believed him, he was sure of that, but she was smart enough not to trust him. This time, he deserved that. Five years ago, especially considering she apparently left him too, he didn't. She finally said, "Before I answer that question, tell me: How did you gain access to the FBI file, considering you don't work for the FBI and you're not on this case?"

He realized the answer wasn't going to help gain her trust. "A buddy I served in the military with now works for the FBI and has been working the case. When Mia was taken, and the CIA wouldn't authorize me to join the case, and the FBI shut me out completely, he gave me access to what he had."

"He could get in a lot of trouble for that," she pointed out.

Rowan inclined his head. "We're both aware, but without the CIA's approval for me to work the case, I have no access." He hesitated, and then continued with a trembling voice. "It's my sister. Those close to me are doing what they can to help." Were there risks? Certainly, but Rowan would risk it all for his military brothers too.

Alex let out another long, deep breath, her eyes searching his while her fingers tapped against the armrest. "I take it the CIA wants you to stay out of this because of your personal relationship?"

He nodded, still frustrated over that call. "That was their decision, yes."

"A decision you obviously don't agree with, since here we are."

Rowan had always followed rules, protocol, authority. The military had raised him into a man. He knew when to talk and when to shut up. But not when it came to his family, blood or otherwise. Everything he honored, believed in, all fell apart when Mia went missing. "There is no rule I won't break to get my sister back. Mia is a sweet girl with her whole life ahead of her. I am her brother, and there is not a damn person who can stop me from trying to find her."

"Even if it costs you your job?"

He gave a firm nod. "Even so."

She tapped her finger against the chair again and exhaled another long, deep breath, both actions of which were tells of hers when she was deep in thought. He'd remembered that from their week together. "I saw in the case files that their suspect list has fizzled out," she finally said. "What do you think I could do to find this person that the FBI hasn't done yet?" Her clever eyes lit up with speculation.

Rowan understood that energy and rush. Hunting killers, running top-secret missions, he got a high from it too. "Every damn thing they haven't tried," he told her simply. "They're not digging deep enough, if you ask me. The killer knows police procedure. The crime scenes are clean. There's no DNA evidence. There's no trail. There's nothing. The only link they've found is that all the victims, including my sister, have used the dating app, SiR, but all the men who had been chatting with the women have been ruled out."

She reached for her laptop again. "But you're suspicious about that?"

Rowan liked that she could read him so well. That was one of the reasons things with Alex were different. No one read him. They couldn't see past his shield. She was the only one, and that had certainly been the biggest reason he'd left her in Paris. She was too close, too dangerous. "The killer is there somewhere on the app," he explained, stretching out his toes that had begun to tingle. "It's the only link between the women. The FBI has missed something, whether they want to admit that or not."

Her fingers began flying across the keyboard, her gaze firmly set on the monitor. "Are you and your sister close?"

"Why is that important to this case?"

Alex's gaze flicked up, and she gave a small smile. "Protective. Okay, so you're close." She glanced back at the monitor and continued typing. "The reason I asked was to find out if she told you anything about the men she dated on the app?"

"Just one."

Alex's fingers froze atop her keyboard. Her eyes searched his, and his expression must have revealed a lot, since she said, "And then she went missing?"

"That's right," he said, having come to the same conclusion she had that the last guy was their suspect. "Mia didn't tell me much about him, except for a few details in passing. They'd been texting back and forth for about a month. She'd never met him in person, and she'd never say much because she signed a nondisclosure agreement that all participants of the app must sign."

Her eyebrows shot up. "An NDA for a dating app?"

"The app connects rich, successful Dominants with submissives," he explained.

"Ah, gotcha," she said, continuing to type on her keyboard. "The men using this app are in powerful positions, I take it?"

Rowan inclined his head. "Men who can't risk their

kinky fetishes being revealed to the public, but I suspect this might be the very reason this case is not getting solved. Money and power can make truth disappear."

Alex nodded in agreement, keeping her gaze on the screen, and moved along. "What else did Mia say about him?"

"She let it slip once that he'd told her he had a military tattoo on his back of a solider with a gas mask and a helicopter beneath it." He remembered that talk so vividly. Could picture his sweet sister with her long blond hair and warm blue eyes smiling at him. "She wondered if I knew him."

"I take it you didn't."

He shook his head.

Alex glanced back to her monitor, her fingers continuing to fly across the keyboard. "All right. Is that it?"

"She told me he says, *balls to the wall.*"

Alex stopped typing again to stare incredulously at him. "Balls to the wall?"

Rowan nodded, stretching out his fingers that were going numb now. "Apparently that's his go-getter saying."

"And just how did *that* come up in a casual conversation?"

Rowan remembered that day in the diner over breakfast. He'd flown in after he worked a case in Portland to spend the day with Mia back home in New York City to catch up. "Mia said it. I called her out on it, then she explained it was something the guy she was talking to texted a lot. She guessed it rubbed off on her."

Alex watched Rowan again intently, obviously things on her mind, before letting out another heavy sigh and typing once more. "Well, it's not a lot to go on, but it's at least some way to identify him." She glanced Rowan's way, setting those pretty, inquisitive eyes on him, making the world disappear a little. "The FBI hasn't been able to locate this guy by those identifying markers? His tattoo sounds unique."

Rowan knew the reaction he was about to get, but he couldn't hold back anything. Not from Alex. Not when he needed her to find Mia. "I haven't told the FBI about the tattoo or the saying."

Her hands dropped flat down on her laptop. "Want to explain why?"

"Because as far as I'm concerned, they're giving me the run-around." Rowan explained the frustration he'd been feeling for days. "This bastard has taken my sister. I stopped playing by the rules when they shut me out, refusing to give me access."

"The FBI and CIA never do work seemingly together, do they?"

"Not even on a good day," Rowan said dryly.

"And especially when they're probably reacting to you telling them they're doing a shitty job."

"They *are* doing a shitty job," Rowan retorted. "My sister is not home safe, and this killer isn't behind bars."

"Valid point," Alex said before turning her focus entirely onto her monitor.

With the reminder of Mia's life on the line, he forged ahead. He considered Alex's mood. Her shoulders were relaxed, posture calm. Now or never. "It's time to answer, Alex. Will you help me? I know this will eat up your vacation—"

"It won't take me that long to find her." Alex made the statement without arrogance, basically stating a fact they both knew was probably true.

While he appreciated her confidence, he snorted. "The FBI can't find this killer."

Her mouth twitched, and her gorgeous eyes flicked to his face. "Why do you think the CIA and FBI keep me in their pockets? I'll find this killer." She placed the laptop aside on the coffee table next to her. "I've got some scripts running on SiR's databases. They'll take a few hours to run before we know anything more, so we'll need to hang tight. But if there is anything to find there, I'll find it."

Rowan realized how much he needed her reassurance. He'd seen Alex work in Paris and catch one of the most ruthless hired hitmen that Rowan had ever heard of. Her legendary hacking skill was not anything he doubted. That brought a sliver of hope that had slowly drained out of him since the FBI hadn't gotten anywhere on finding his sister in the last week. He became hyperaware he was still tied to the damn chair, and very much at her disposal. "While I appreciate your help, do you ever plan to untie me?"

"Not yet," she stated, giving him firm eye contact. "Since this isn't a CIA or FBI op, I don't work for free."

He breathed deep, albeit surprised she wanted money. She never seemed the material type. He had a good fifty grand in his savings account that came from years of working instead of living, and he'd give it all to her. "What's your price?"

She held his stare in an intense way he'd never seen from a woman before. She had no fear, total confidence, and fuck, was she sexy. She bit her lip, drawing his entire focus to her mouth, and his cock hardened that easily. That's what had fascinated him back in Paris. His control was ironclad. Except when it came to this twenty-seven-year-old, five-foot-four fireball of a brunette. "The way I see this," she said with a sexy smile, "you have taken the vacation that I desperately needed and stolen it away. You need to rectify that."

Rowan felt his muscles quiver in need. He wanted her as much now as when he first set his eyes on her in Paris. And he wasn't a man who didn't indulge when life put a sexy woman in front of him. He saw the worst in people. He dealt in murder, misery, and lies. He took the good when he could, and he never apologized for it. "And how shall I rectify that, luv?"

She leaned forward a little, showing a hint of cleavage through the opening of her robe. "We'll get to that, but first, I need to be clear about a few things. Before you woke up, I had a call with my boss, Ryder Blackwood, whom I'm guessing you probably know about."

"I'm aware of him, yes." Blackwood was a retired Army Ranger. Apparently, he'd taught her to protect herself. But deep down, Rowan thought a lot of what Alex could do was a result of her instincts. Before he met her in Paris, he'd seen the CIA videos of them interviewing her as a teenager. Plus, he'd witnessed it in her during their seven days together. He liked her smart mouth, as much as he liked her sharp mind.

"Good," she went on. "I showed Ryder your face and explained the situation." She looked as if she wanted to ravish him and bury him both at once. "Not only is he checking into you now, but Ryder and I are very close. Put me in any danger, and he will kill you."

"I have no intention of hurting you," Rowan told her gently, noting the sudden shift in her mood. He caught the building heat in her eyes, telling him her mind was now on something else entirely. And he understood the need to dip into this passion. There was an energy between them. A pulse that only seemed to intensify since he'd been bound to this chair. Wanting to play along and show her he wanted exactly what he expected she did, he gestured to his bindings. "In fact, if you take these off, I'll show you just how good I want to make you feel."

A building smile rose to her face as she stood, her robe coming undone a little more, showing off her lacy bra. "We haven't negotiated those terms yet." She moved to her purse and reached for something inside. When she turned back, he realized she held onto a condom. "While those scripts run, let's negotiate, shall we?"

Blood filled his cock so fast, making him so hard, he bit back a groan. "Name your terms."

She watched him for a long moment, giving him a very thorough once-over that caused quivering in his muscles before she moved to the closet. When she turned around, she held a black scarf in her hands and sent her robe to the floor. "No one keeps me in the dark, Hawke." She stalked forward, wearing only her lingerie. He hungered for her, building deep in his gut, until a growl spilled from his chest as she went on. "Secrets are things I find out." When she stopped in front of him, she tied the makeshift blindfold around his head. "Do you like being in the dark, Hawke?" she whispered huskily in his ear.

He gritted his teeth at his erection pressing against his jeans. "I'd rather see all of you," he muttered.

She gave a soft, throaty laugh that had his cock jerking, but then she grabbed his chin firmly and declared, "Keep secrets from me again, and you better get used to this darkness because I'll erase you. For good."

A ragged groan was yanked from deep in his chest when she opened his jeans and shoved them down enough to free his throbbing cock. His eyes rolled back into his head when she applied the condom, stroking him perfectly, all to tease. He forced words out from deep in his throat. "Are those your terms, Alex? No more secrets between us?"

Her thighs brushed across his legs when she straddled him, and he grunted when she pressed herself against the tip of him. "The terms are this: Don't cross me. Don't lie to me again. No tricks. It won't end well for you. Understand?"

"Goddamn it." He groaned, tortured by her closeness. "Yes. Fuck me."

A second later, she was all around him, and he tossed his head back at the pleasure, releasing a groan at how tight and perfect she was. Even better than he remembered. He fisted his hands, straining against the bindings, knowing they wouldn't break. She took his mouth and kissed him fiercely, cupping his face and riding his cock like she'd been starved of him.

And, fuck, he felt starved of her.

Every grind of her hips drove his pleasure higher. He'd never been bound or blindfolded, and his senses were heightened. Everything felt alive. His skin tingled. He felt her harsh breathy moans against his lips. He felt the quivers of her heat in her building pleasure. He smelled her, their sex, and the intensity was drawing his balls up close to his body, ready to explode.

She pulled ragged grunts deep from his chest with every thrust of her hips. He ached to blow at each moan she gave. Until she moved harder, faster, threading her fingers into his bound hands and holding onto him like she owned him. Like she'd been craving him for the last five years and finally let herself go again now that she'd had him close.

And damn, he felt that too.

"Alex," he grunted, as heat flooded his lower half, stealing his control. Beneath the blindfold, he went cross-eyed from the pleasure.

She froze.

"Fucking hell." He dropped his head back and gritted his teeth as his dick pulsed, no doubt pre-cum leaking out, right on the very edge of his climax.

She removed the blindfold, and then he was lost in her gorgeous eyes. This blindingly breathtaking, dark-haired beauty that only made the pause in the pleasure torturous. "Let there be no misunderstanding, Hawke," she said firmly, pink dusting her cheeks. "I own this show. Clear?"

He'd say anything to ensure she moved again. "Yeah,

McCoy, we're clear." He meant those words for the few seconds before she locked her hooded eyes on him and thrust her hips until they were both bucking and jerking their pleasure, free-falling into the place they were so beautiful together.

Tomorrow, though, it'd be another story.

# CHAPTER 4

"**H**AVE YOU LOST your fucking mind?"

"Good morning to you too." Alex smiled at Ryder's near-snarl through her computer monitor. She sat on her bed cross-legged, watching her programs continue to comb through SiR's databases searching out possible suspects. After having more sex than she'd had in the past five years, she was sore in all the right places from a wild night with Rowan. "Do you have anything to report?

Ryder's frown only deepened. "You slept with Hawke."

"Wait...*what*? How did you...?" Her eyes slowly narrowed as Ryder began looking everywhere but at her. "You know I *hate* when you have anyone watch me," she snapped.

His gaze flicked by hers. "I was concerned for your safety and have had eyes on you ever since we talked last night."

"Whose eyes?" She jumped off the bed, leaving her laptop there, hearing Ryder's heavy sigh. She shoved the curtain aside and peered out the window, only finding another building across the street. One of Ryder's men could be anywhere. They were like ghosts. Always there, but you could never see them. The only place they wouldn't find her was on her laptop. No one could hack her. She'd be alerted before anyone got close.

"It's someone I trust," Ryder called. She returned to the bed, pulling her laptop onto her lap again, ready to rip into him, when he interjected in his firm voice, "Now back to what really matters here. Have I taught you nothing?"

This was her first assignment that wasn't run by the FBI or CIA or Ryder, but she didn't feel she'd taken too many missteps yet. Well, except for sleeping with the guy who tried to play her, but she had good reasons for that. One, she did actually believe what he told her. The FBI files on the case told her that much. Two, she couldn't quite control herself either when it came to Rowan. Instead of fighting the lust burning between them, she went with it to make something of her vacation. At least she'd go home riding an orgasm high, and if she could help him find his sister, she would.

"Stop looking at me like that," she defended, the mattress bouncing beneath her as she settled her back against the pillows. "We just slept together. It's not like I proposed marriage." When Ryder's expression only darkened, she added, "I'm safe and alive, as you can see."

"You shouldn't have done anything with him," Ryder rebuked, his face drawing closer to the monitor. "What if he meant to hurt you?"

"Then he would've hurt me the moment we got into the hotel room," she countered. "Besides, I *know* him, remember? His sister is one of the victims, like I told you in my text message. He only wants to find her." Alex gave him an easy smile, hoping that softened him up. "Not that I don't appreciate the big brother act, but let's stay focused on what *actually* matters here. Have you learned something about Rowan that poses a problem, and that's where all this is coming from?"

"First, tell me what he's told you," Ryder said.

The ease in Ryder's jawline told her she had nothing to worry about when it came to Rowan, so she gave Ryder what he wanted. "Here's what I know so far…" She laid out all the facts that Rowan had explained to her about the case. They'd gone through the FBI files again last night after she untied him from the chair. Nothing appeared odd, but something didn't feel right either. That was never a good sign.

When she finished laying out all the facts, Ryder arched an eyebrow. "And that's it?"

"That's it." She nodded.

Ryder's mouth pinched—his classic move for when something felt off to him too—before he addressed her again. "Is Hawke still gone?"

Alex drew in a long, deep breath to attempt not to yell at him, since apparently Ryder knew Rowan had left to grab them breakfast. Alex's scripts were taking longer than usual, and when Rowan began pacing, obviously deeply concerned for his sister, Alex gave him a job. She needed food, and so did he. They both needed to stay sharp and energized to see this through. "Listen, I love you, I do, but get those eyes off me now or I'll shut your system down and keep it down until you stop having me watched."

Ryder's gaze searched hers for a long moment, and then he cursed and shook his head. "I don't like this, Alex." She wisely stayed silent as he sat back in his chair and crossed his arms, looking like the mighty solider he was. "Hawke has already misled you once."

"Yes, I know, but…" She hesitated then laid everything on the line. "If this were you, I would do everything I could to help you. Rowan is a sneaky CIA agent, yes, but he also just wants to find his sister. We both know I am the best one to help find this killer. Rowan and I…there's history there, and it's good history." Especially considering she'd always thought in that moment of weakness where her heart felt all exposed, she'd run out on him. Apparently, she hadn't been the only one shaken by their week together.

Good to know.

"Then why didn't he just tell you that in the first place?"

*Because he thought I hated him for leaving me...* "Because I'm so damn irresistible." She grinned.

Ryder scoffed, though the joke worked its magic and he gave a half smile. "Just be careful with this one. Hawke typically works deep undercover. Confirming his identity came at a price. Most files on him at the CIA have been buried."

Alex instantly cringed. "Do I want to know that price?"

A hint of a grin lifted the corners of Ryder's mouth. "You owe a favor."

*To the CIA* was what Ryder didn't say. "I hope I don't regret that."

"You and me both," Ryder agreed. "I know why you're doing this, Alex." Yeah, Alex knew something about losing a sister, and she'd been on a mission to save as many people as she could to fill in that dark hole that came from the inability to save Lena, but Alex really didn't want to talk about that as Ryder went on. "I also know that's the only reason you didn't kick Hawke's stupid ass out for not being upfront right away. But this girl is not your sister."

Alex wouldn't even pretend that a little part of her didn't think of Lena now. Alex always tried to fix that wrong. "I'm not on a personal quest here. Besides, the way I see it, I'm the only way to find Hawke's sister. I think that provides me some level of control here, don't you?"

"Just making sure you realize the stakes," Ryder said.

The door suddenly opened, and Rowan walked in. All man, jeans, and a leather jacket... Sweet Jesus, she nearly drooled. Rowan was danger and sex all rolled up into hard muscle. He carried a tray of coffees and a paper bag, and met her with a warm smile. Obviously not realizing she was on a call, he said, "You can't come to New York City and not have a crème brûlée danish. Figured you probably wanted a coffee too. Still take it with one milk?"

"Suck up," Ryder muttered.

Rowan froze, now aware they weren't alone in the room before setting everything down on the coffee table.

When Rowan handed her a coffee, Ryder said, "Let me talk to him."

Rowan smiled. The type of smile that was challenging, deadly, and screamed testosterone.

"Play nice, boys," Alex told them both before she turned the monitor to face Rowan.

They both promptly ignored her.

"You know who I am," Ryder stated.

Rowan inclined his head, his gaze turning harder than she'd seen before, making her realize he softened a lot when he looked at her. "You know who I am," Rowan retorted.

"I'm aware," Ryder said. "No games, Hawke. Any sign that Alex is in danger, she'll be pulled out."

Rowan's hair fell down his jawline, and Alex tried desperately not to want to kiss along that sculpted line. She barely resisted, her lips twitching to press right *there,* when Rowan said, "The goal here is to save lives, not lose them."

A heavy pause. Then Ryder's voice firmed. "Trick her again and you'll regret it."

Rowan didn't even hesitate. "If it were your sister...or your wife"—Alex flinched, picturing the intensity filling Ryder's expression at the mention of *wife*—"you would stop at nothing to find them either."

"Which is the only reason you're not dead."

At that, Rowan's eyes narrowed into slits. "You could try, Blackwood."

Most times, Alex knew Ryder wasn't serious when he threatened to take someone out, but sometimes she got the feeling that if pressed, he'd do so without hesitation.

In some weird way, that made her feel safe, even though morally, to like such a thing felt terribly wrong.

Ryder's voice tightened. "One misstep and this is over."

Alex rolled her eyes and sighed heavily so they both heard her. "All right, that's enough testosterone for one morning." She didn't need either man telling her what she could or couldn't do. "I'll reach out if I need anything," she told Ryder.

The hardness around Ryder's mouth was indication

enough that he hated the idea that he wasn't involved. She quickly added, "I'll be safe. Promise."

Ryder watched her a moment, his jaw muscles clenching. "I'd like to keep eyes on you—"

"Goodbye, Ryder." She ended the chat, hearing his curse as he faded away. Regardless of what she said, she knew Ryder would keep those eyes on her, even if she told him not to. Only he'd ensure she never found out about it. Not that she could really blame him. Hell, she'd probably do the same thing too.

"He's protective of you," Rowan said, offering her the danish.

She stared at the most delicious display of sugar and bread in one mouth-watering pastry. "We've been a team for a really long time. We're like family."

Rowan grabbed the chair in the corner of the room and pulled it closer to the bed before sitting down. He rested his elbows on his knees and gave her a steady look. "I won't let you get hurt, Alex. I hope you know that."

"For both our sakes, you better not." She took a bite of the pastry and nearly melted as the sweetness lingered against her tongue. "Dear God, that is delicious," she said after swallowing the bite. "Thank you."

He smiled. "You're welcome." Then he sipped his coffee.

She licked her fingers then focused back onto her laptop. "While you were gone, I got us some names that stood out—names, by the way, that are not on the FBI's suspect list."

"How many names?" he asked, eyebrows raised.

"Two," she answered, taking another bite of her danish. "One had direct contact with all the deceased women, plus the two other missing women and your sister."

"How about the other name?"

"He didn't talk directly to your sister. She ignored his message. But he's ex-military, so it's still good to check him out."

Rowan nodded. "I agree. And what of their tattoos? Any hits there?"

"I scoured the internet," she explained. "I couldn't find a photograph of either man with their shirt off or a mention of the tattoo online."

"All right." Rowan hesitated, looking down at the paper cup in his hand, the sunlight from the window creating a soft glow on his face.

The silence grew daunting. "What is it?"

He glanced up through his lashes. "Do you find it odd that you easily found two suspects the FBI over-looked?"

She pondered that through a sip of her coffee then finally decided. "Sure, I'd like to think I'm just that good, but it is strange that the FBI's cyber division didn't pull these names. Of course, they didn't know about the military angle, but they should have stood out."

Rowan gave a slow nod. "Which is exactly what I've been bumping up against time and time again. Something about this entire case feels…*off.* The work seems shoddy."

Alex stuffed another piece of danish into her mouth and murmured, "Any idea why?"

"No," Rowan said with obvious frustration. He ran his hand across his eyes then straightened up and asked, "What comes next?"

"I'll need your credit card."

He arched an eyebrow. "For?"

"The first possible suspect is Brett Manning." She explained what she'd learned before Ryder called. "He's a pilot who owns a private airfield, which actually benefits us here because we can use him to fly us to Seattle to meet our second possible suspect, Heath Lennox. He's a billionaire and puts on a snazzy charity masquerade ball every year that just so happens to be tonight." She turned the laptop screen toward Rowan. "Here's Brett's schedule. All I need to do is rework things a bit and get us in there, and we're a go."

"You can do that?" he asked.

She smiled. "I can do anything, but it's going to cost you. You've got savings you can dip into?"

"Yeah, I got some. My father knew a thing or two about investing." He reached for his pocket and pulled out his wallet. "All right, do it."

She tapped the enter button on her keyboard. "Done."

He slowly looked up, frowned. "I didn't give you my credit card?"

"Yeah, well, I got that this morning." She avoided his slight scowl, and went on, "We'll land in Seattle in six hours. That gives us three hours to shop and an hour for my hair and makeup."

He narrowed his eyes. "Don't you think you're milking this a bit?"

"It's a formal affair," she said with no hint of remorse. "You'll need a tux too." She continued typing, adding them onto the masquerade party's guest list. "We need to pretend to belong with the top one percent. Besides, I must look my absolute best."

"You look just fine like this," he said, his gaze raking over her.

She squirmed against the heat his intense regard scorched through her. "Yeah, but we need to make me look spectacular."

His brow arched again. "And why is that?"

She smiled. "Because I need to be the *only* woman at the ball that Lennox sees."

# CHAPTER 5

A N HOUR LATER, Rowan followed Alex into a
boutique shop on Fifth Avenue. The shop was tiny.
The price tags on the dresses were not, but all that
mattered was Mia. He hadn't once let himself think
about the fear his baby sister must be enduring, though
his sister was tough, and he knew she'd keep her smarts
about her until he got there. He only needed to keep
moving forward, closing the gap between where she was
kept and where he stood. Failure wasn't an option. Their
flight to Seattle was in an hour, and they needed to dress
the part for the ball. Rowan had quickly rented a tux that
fit him well enough. Alex had spent the last hour dress
shopping, and when he found her, she looked more than
frustrated.

She reached for a long black dress, but Rowan knew
that was all wrong. "Not that one." He glanced around
and spotted a slinky cherry-red gown. "This one is
Lennox's flavor."

"How do you know that?" Alex asked, taking the
hanger from him, studying the dress intently.

"After I picked up my tux, I looked into him," Rowan explained, leaning a shoulder against the wall. The sales lady walked in their direction, but Rowan smiled and politely waved her off, wanting this conversation to stay private. When she moved along to another customer, he continued with Alex. "Every woman that I've seen Lennox photographed with is always wearing a red dress. Which tells me it's his preference."

"Then let's go with that." Alex turned toward the dressing room, but Rowan reached for her arm.

"Lennox won't be the only one looking at you in that dress, Alex." He caught the hitch of her breath and the dilation of her eyes, and his cock swiftly hardened.

She gave a soft, sexy smile that belonged to *him*—that Lennox would not see tonight. "Let's just hope he feels the same way you do."

"He's a man," Rowan stated. "He'll notice you."

She didn't respond and moved toward the changing room. When she reached the red curtain, she glanced back over her shoulder. "And what about hair? What's Lennox's preference there?"

"Up," Rowan told her.

But that wasn't for Lennox. That was all for him.

The thoughts of her long neck and back beautifully exposed stayed with Rowan the rest of the day, as did his semi, until they arrived later that afternoon to the private airport in a stretch limousine. No expense had been spared to play the part of a rich couple going on a date night to Seattle. Rowan wouldn't make one wrong move, not with Mia's life on the line. He felt so close to the killer, he could taste it, and that meant that soon his sister would be home and safe. The private airport had three small jets on the tarmac. Only one of those planes had a pilot standing near the staircase, with a flight attendant next to him. "I take it that's our ride?" Rowan asked.

Alex nodded, her sharp eyes on her target. "Yeah, that's him. Brett Manning."

Rowan met the limo driver at the trunk and took out their suitcase for the night. He tipped the driver before he placed his hand on the small of Alex's back, guiding her toward the plane. He was not blind to how much he enjoyed touching her, and by her slight shiver, how she reciprocated that sentiment. That obviously hadn't changed between them over the years.

As they approached the plane, Alex commented, "He doesn't look like a killer."

"Serial killers never look like killers," Rowan replied. "That's what makes them so dangerous."

She acknowledged his remark with a shrug.

Rowan studied Manning as they drew closer. He exhaled deeply, trying not to let his emotions run away with him. For all he knew, he was looking at the very man who abducted his sister and planned on killing her.

Manning wore a jacket, leaving Rowan unable to look for the tattoo, but he kept his focus sharp and watched for any and all body language the man put off.

Manning took a big deep breath and gave them an award-winning smile, dipping his chin slightly. "Mr. Hawke and Ms. McCoy?"

"Yes, that's right." Rowan offered his hand. "Thank you for arranging this flight for us on such short notice." They could have given false names, but getting identification took time. Time that they didn't have. Rowan knew their arrival set off alarms at the CIA headquarters, but seeing that his boss had known about Rowan's intimate relationship in Paris, Rowan suspected the CIA would overlook his travels with her.

"It's not a problem," Manning said, avoiding Rowan's stare, and then included Alex in the conversation. "And you're just in Seattle for the night?"

"We are, thank you," Alex said, then boarded the plane like she owned it. "We must get going immediately or we'll be late for our plans tonight."

"Yes, miss, of course. We'll get up in the air as quick as we can." Manning's shoulder curled a little when he gestured Rowan into the plane.

Rowan hurried up the few steps and walked into luxury. Leather seats. A big-screen television. Under different circumstances, Rowan would make full use of this plane for his enjoyment, but he forced his mind clear.

He took a seat across from an already-settled Alex. She smiled at him; obviously her bravado was a show of a person who demanded excellence. This flight was costing Rowan ten grand, but there was no cost he wouldn't pay if it brought him closer to finding Mia.

"What do you make of him?" Alex asked, after the flight attendant boarded the plane and moved toward the cabin, packing away the suitcase.

"I take him for an anxious sort," Rowan said. "His shoulders slightly curved when he talked to us. There was a dip of his chin when you got pushy. And I saw him taking repeated deep breaths."

Alex's brows drew together. "How do you even see all that?"

He buckled up his seat belt, watching her do the same. "It's my job to see these little things and know how to read people. It's the only way to stay a step ahead of them. It's these subtle cues that will tell you more about someone than anything that comes out of their mouth."

Her brows tightened further. "What did you read off me?"

"You might be the one and only person I have a hard time reading," he said with a dry laugh. "You were a complete surprise and bulldozed over any control of the situation that I had."

She smiled softly, telling him she didn't mind that

one bit. "So, about those little cues, what's your gut say about this guy?"

"That he's not our guy," Rowan stated.

Alex snorted a laugh. "That sure, are you?"

Rowan nodded. "He's too nervous."

"But maybe that's why he kills. To take control of that nervousness."

Rowan shrugged. "Always a possibility, but he's not the type of guy I would see my sister being interested in. Manning barely looked me in the eye. He's timid. Mia hates weakness."

Alex eventually agreed with a nod and then turned to the flight attendant who sidled up next to them. Her navy-blue blazer and skirt were so neat that Rowan couldn't find a single wrinkle. Her blond hair was pulled up in a tight bun, without a strand out of place. And her makeup was flawless. *Samantha* was on her nametag. "Can I get you anything to drink?"

"A coffee with milk, please," Alex said.

Rowan gave a nod. "I'll take black."

"Excellent," Samantha said with a beaming smile. "Once we're up in the air, I'll get those right to you."

In the same moment she turned away, Manning strode out from the cabin with a matching smile to Samantha's and his jacket nowhere in sight. "We're just about to taxi down the runway here. I hope you both have an enjoyable flight. If you need anything, please don't hesitate to ask Samantha, your flight attendant."

"Thank you," Rowan replied. He held his breath and waited for Manning to turn away. Through the light fabric of Manning's shirt, it became clear he did not have a back tattoo. He turned to Alex and sighed. "One down."

She nodded. "That may have been the quickest ruling out a suspect I've ever been a part of."

"You and me both," Rowan agreed with a laugh. "Usually clearing suspects is much more painful." He had the scars to prove it.

The plane soon taxied down the runway and was off the ground not long after that. Rowan stared out his window, looking at the city disappearing below them until they were over dark blue water.

"You never mentioned you had a sister."

Alex's soft voice pulled him back to her. He noted the slight hurt in her expression that she tried very hard to hide. "I don't talk about Mia to anyone," he explained gently. "In my line of work, she'd be the first person that someone would go after to hurt me."

"Makes sense."

But it still hurt her. He saw that.

The aroma of brewing coffee filled the cabin when she finally looked his way again. "How are your parents doing? Are they still living in Vermont?"

It surprised him that he had mentioned them to her

in Paris. He couldn't recall that conversation, and as much as he didn't talk about Mia, he also usually didn't talk about his parents, but it only reminded him how different Alex had been to him. He shared things he never shared with anyone. "Sailing the Pacific at the moment."

Alex smiled. "That's good to hear." Then her smile faded. "Do they know Mia is missing?"

He shook his head. "One perk of being in the CIA. I've gotten her name kept out of the media and bought some time with the Feds before they reach out to them. I don't want to worry them. I'll find her." He *had* to find her. He couldn't fathom any other outcome.

Silence filled the space between them as Rowan stared into Alex's warm eyes. The level of comfort with her had not changed. Intimacy was such a foreign thing. Through all the girlfriends he had in the past, none made him feel so at ease and turned on as Alex. In Paris, he thought Alex's draw was her wit, her strength, and her abilities. Now, five years later, he knew it had to be something more. Something that only she possessed, whatever that may be. At some point, he needed to find out exactly what had such a grip on him. But it occurred to him that unlike five years ago, this awareness didn't shake him. She made him curious.

"You're right—*we* will find her."

Rowan blinked out of his thoughts and found she'd

come to sit next to him. "Mia," Alex continued. "We'll find her before it's too late. I promise."

Warmth touched his chest. He reached for Alex's hand and kissed her knuckles. "You'll find her, luv."

A slow, dangerous smile filled Alex's face. "And you'll kill him."

Rowan let the silence be his answer. He glanced past her, out the window. The kind thing would be a quick kill for the man who took so many innocent lives for his twisted sadistic games.

Kindness was not Rowan's strong suit.

He was so deep in his thoughts that he hadn't realized the flight attendant had delivered their coffees, and only blinked back into awareness when Alex rose.

"Be back in a few," she said before heading down the aisle to the bathroom.

Rowan sipped his coffee, knowing the six-hour flight would feel long. The bitter coffee hit his taste buds, providing just the bite he needed. Though the more he sat there, watching the flight attendant busying herself with preparing their food, the more he realized he wanted to taste something more than coffee.

He took one final sip of his coffee, leaving it on the small table next to his seat, then he followed to where Alex had gone. For this one moment, he let Mia go from his mind, and allowed himself to dip into something good. He stopped outside the door and knocked. The door slowly opened.

Alex grinned. "You took way too long." She grabbed his shirt and pulled him in and quickly locked the door behind him.

She looked hot, eager, and turned on when he grasped her hips, placing her against the sink. The toilet was behind him. The shower to his left. And the amount of space in the bathroom was comparable to the bathroom in Alex's hotel room. He caught her licking her lips as he lifted the front of her shirt enough to unbutton her jeans. Her gaze heated beautifully when he tucked his fingers into the rim of her panties, and pulled those, along with her jeans, down until she was stepping out of her shoes, then her pants. Only when he had her bottom half bared did he cup her neck, lifting her chin up with his thumb, and sealed his mouth across hers. He gave her long, slow kisses, savoring each and every one. She moaned against his lips when he kicked open her legs and slid his fingers between her thighs, finding her already wet. He loved that about her. How ready she always was for him.

It made them even. He was always hard.

"You feel so damn good, luv," he murmured against her lips.

She moaned in return. He stroked the silkiness of her arousal and drew it up over her clit, while he swirled the bud, feeling the tremble of her leg against his thigh.

"Rowan," she breathed.

"Say that again." He leaned away, threaded his fingers into her hair, staring into her hooded eyes.

"Rowan."

"Christ, I love how that sounds coming from your mouth." Heat consumed him, pulling him deeper under her spell when he pressed his mouth against hers again and kissed her roughly, swirling her into pleasure with every hard press of his fingers, until she moaned louder. Then, and only then, did he drop to one knee. He kissed her thigh and heard her sharp intake of breath as he draped her thigh over his shoulder. Teasing her, he gently licked her soft folds. She slid her hands into his hair, tipped her head back, and moaned deeply.

He played, tickled, teased, until she began trembling.

After that, he gave her what she wanted from him. A body-quivering orgasm that had her standing up on her tiptoes and screaming his name.

He wasted no time exposing his cock, applying a condom, and then sinking himself deep inside of her hot and wet sex. She was primed and ready, and he gave it to her hard, exactly how he knew they both liked it.

She stared into his eyes while he took her, giving all of herself, and he took everything she had to give him. Until they were both falling into pleasure. Her first, then he followed, bucking and jerking with his climax.

She sagged against the mirror behind her, with her

sweet ass still resting on the sink.

He withdrew his cock, disposed of the condom, then spun her around. "What are you doing…?" She gasped as he slapped her ass. Hard.

"We've got six hours before we land." He pressed against her back, bent her across the sink, dropped to one knee again behind her, and treated himself to *her* all over again. Her quivering moan echoed around him as he said, "I'm nowhere near done with you."

And he wasn't sure he'd ever be.

# CHAPTER 6

J UST AFTER EIGHT o'clock at night, in the heart of
downtown Seattle, Alex left the spa she'd been
spending the last three hours at getting spoiled rotten.
The cherry-red, satin mermaid gown fit her like a glove
in all the right places. Maybe there was something to
being fussed over. She felt a little like a woman in some
fairy tale she never believed in before. Her makeup was
flawless, her lipstick perfectly matched her dress, and her
hair was done in a soft romantic updo that was somehow
gentle, sexy, and beautiful all at once. Only this fairy tale
included a sadistic killer, five deceased women, and three
more missing women—one of them Rowan's beloved
sister. Kinda hard to get all swoony knowing what
exactly brought Alex there tonight.

When the spa's door swooshed closed behind her,
she noticed the sun sitting a little lower in the sky. But
another view quickly dominated. Rowan was leaning
against the limo, glancing down at his phone. He wore a
tux and his hair was gelled back, not a strand out of
place. Rowan held a lethal edge, and Alex didn't doubt

that if his deadly switch got flicked, Rowan could kill easily. For reasons she couldn't quite figure out, seeing someone so dangerous, all cleaned up, brought uncontrollable heat low in her body.

Rowan looked very *hot* and very *male.*

When she drew close, he slowly looked up and gave a blinding smile. She liked both the instant surprise and heat in his eyes. "Yeah, I know," she said playfully. "I'm killing it in this dress."

Rowan chuckled then took the two long steps to meet her halfway. The air shifted when he got in close, and she felt the hot shiver slide over her when he dragged a hand across her lower exposed back, bringing her in tight against the hard lines of his body. "That dress is going to kill *me.*" As if it was fully his right to do so, he kissed her. She'd like to think that she could pull back at any minute and stop, but she'd fail if she tried.

Intensity and lust, and something she couldn't even understand, passed between them when his lips pressed intimately against hers. And when he cupped her face and deepened the kiss, she lost herself completely.

By the time he broke away, they were both breathing heavily. Horns honking, brakes squealing, a couple laughing as they walked by, all engulfed Alex again while she caught the smolder in Rowan's eyes.

He kept his mouth close to hers while he trailed his thumb gingerly down the side of her neck. "You're making it very difficult for me to remember the reasons we are here."

"Just keeping you on your toes, Hawke." She smiled, and then she strode around him, but damn, she was shaken. No man could make her lose herself like Rowan could. Five years ago, that terrified her. It *still* terrified her. She got into the back of the limo, leaving the door open, and Rowan joined her, sliding against the leather seat until his thigh pressed against hers.

He shut the door then gestured at the driver, who quickly drove off and slid the privacy divider up.

Alex glanced out the window and drew in couple of stabilizing breaths to shed the remaining heat, quickly re-applying her lipstick. The evening had been full of relaxation, but the reminder that she could be meeting a killer alone tonight made her tense.

"You're nervous," Rowan said, scooping up her hand and tangling his fingers with hers. "Don't be."

She glanced his way and snorted. "In case you forgot, I'm the one typically behind the computer screen, not the one talking to possible killers."

Rowan acknowledged her concern with a gentle nod. "I'll be there with you." He reached into his pocket then and handed her a two-way earpiece. "I've got mine." He tapped his right ear. "I'll be close. Always."

"Thank you." Alex accepted the earpiece with a smile and then placed it inside her ear before addressing

Rowan again. "What do I need to know about Lennox?" Rowan had told her when he dropped her off at the spa that he would research him further.

"He's definitely the Dominant type," Rowan said. "So, as much as you can, entice him by being demure and submissive."

Well, if that wasn't a sure way to ruin the fairy-tale buzz. "You do realize how difficult that's going to be for me?"

"I do," he acknowledged with a nod. "But Lennox will be drawn to a woman with submissive traits. Wait until you catch his eye, then cast your gaze down and smile shyly. Allow him to have his ego and the control."

"I think I'm going to be sick," Alex grumbled.

The limo slowed, obviously at a red light as Rowan chuckled. "You'll do fine." He reached into his left pocket then offered her what looked like an EpiPen, only half the size. "Since you seem to enjoy knocking people out, use that on Lennox after you get him alone, then we can check for the tattoo."

She accepted the auto-injector and tucked it away in her clutch. "You've got all the toys, huh?"

"The best ones." He grinned.

Yeah, he wasn't talking about toys from the CIA anymore.

Before she could respond, his sly smile faded as he reached into his other pocket and pulled out his phone and then handed it to Alex again. "That's the target. Have you got him memorized?"

Alex studied the photograph. Heath Lennox was gorgeous. Tall, dark, and handsome, with a body thrown in there that she didn't doubt was ripped and strong. He definitely was the type of man that stood out. "Yeah, I've got him."

"Good." Rowan accepted the phone back and returned it to his pocket as the limo drove off again, picking up speed. "We're going to drop you off first. Get a drink before you do anything, to give me time to get in there. I'm going to have the driver circle the block once before bringing me back."

"Okay." She drew in another deep breath, readying herself.

The limo took three more right turns and then pulled to a stop. Press swarmed, which wasn't all that much of a surprise considering how wealthy Lennox was. Celebrities would likely be at the party, as would the city's politicians showing their support to Lennox's cause. She reached for the door handle to open the door when Rowan stopped her by grabbing her hand.

"Don't forget this." He reached across the seat and grabbed a small box and then opened it. Her heart fluttered at the gorgeous red and black metal mask. Elegant and sexy, she couldn't help but admire the feminine lines of the mask before Rowan helped tie it around her head. When she glanced back at him, he scanned her face and then he gave her a panty-dropping smile. "Gorgeous."

Warmth touched her heart...and every other place craving Rowan's touch. "Keep me safe tonight, Hawke, and you might just see me in *only* this mask."

He gripped her chin and dropped a hard kiss on her mouth. "That's a promise, McCoy." When he broke the kiss, she went to move away, but he kept his hold tight on her chin. His eyes were warm and soft, both very unlike him. "Thank you, Alex. For helping me find Mia."

Her heart did something weird in her chest. Got all tingly. "You would have done the same thing for me." She began to open the door but someone outside opened it farther. She stepped outside and said, "Thank you" to the man in the tux, and then she turned toward the grand 1930s European-style hotel. The limo drove off behind her as she passed beneath the American flag. The doorman held the door open for her as she strode inside. It came as no surprise that she immediately met security. Lennox was a billionaire and had likely rented out the entire hotel for the event.

"Name," the security guy, wearing a black suit, asked.

She pulled her identification from her clutch. "Alex McCoy." Of course, she felt horrible for taking another couple off the list to use their spots, but if it saved their lives and got Rowan his sister back, then it was worth it. And Alex promised to donate to the cause after Mia was back home, since the other couple likely would have donated too.

The security scanned her ID, waited for the loud beep, and then gave a polite smile. "Enjoy your evening, Ms. McCoy."

"Thank you."

Leaving the security behind her, she strode down the long hallway, with the orchestra playing classical music drawing her forward. Not a dozen steps later, she entered the ballroom and found that Lennox had gone to every expense. Crystal chandeliers hung from the high ceilings. Waiters and waitresses strode around the room, some offering glasses of champagne and hors d'oeuvres. The partygoers, all wearing masquerade masks, were mingling by the bar or standing with groups at the round tables with black linens and large feather centerpieces.

Alex moved to the bar. She caught the eye of a bartender who immediately came over to her. "Apple martini, please," she ordered.

"Coming right up." The bartender gave her a sinful smile, indicating that Rowan got the dress just right.

Hell, even she knew he got the dress right, but she also didn't want anyone else looking at her in this dress other than Rowan...and that was an obvious problem.

They'd been in this exact spot before; she cared too much when it came to Rowan.

Last time, she ran.

Maybe it helped knowing he'd been just as unsure back then.

When the bartender delivered the martini, Alex set thoughts of Rowan to the back of her mind and took a long sip to ease her nerves, then scanned the ballroom. The sparkles of diamonds around women's necks and wrists and fingers glistened against the overhead lighting coming off the chandeliers. The ballroom reeked of wealth and status, and Alex had never felt more uncomfortable in her life. She'd never known this world, and only tasted lavish living when Ryder would invite her to parties that he'd attend for politicians or celebrities when he got suckered into it.

"You need to relax." Rowan's smooth voice came across the earpiece. "You look wound up tightener than a clock."

"I can think of a way to fix that," she replied, holding her glass at her mouth to keep the conversation private. But she knew it wasn't only the atmosphere making her uneasy; it was familiarity of how she felt with Rowan. They were almost repeating history, and this time she felt herself wanting to stick more than she had before. His vulnerability about his sister opened him up and caused a rush of feelings in her that made her weak. She hated weakness. "Do you see Lennox?" she asked, getting on task.

"He's at your three o'clock."

Alex followed Rowan's direction, and indeed, she found Heath Lennox, standing by a large ice sculpture, with two ladies at his side. Not just any women. These ladies looked like they belonged on the Victoria's Secret runway. "You expect me to compete with *that*?"

Rowan didn't even hesitate. "First of all, you're not giving yourself enough credit. Those women there are not you."

Her heart just about melted into a pile of goo before she got control of it. "Laying it on thick, Hawke."

"Always, McCoy," Rowan said.

She searched to find him in the crowd, but he wasn't near the dance floor or the bar. A CIA agent doing what he did best, she figured. Staying hidden.

"Second," Rowan continued, "those women are for show. Neither are a breathtakingly stunning submissive in a red dress. Why don't you go and demurely circle Lennox so he takes notice of you?"

*Get in, get out.* That's what Ryder always said. He never delayed any assignment. He acted quick and decisively. Leaning on his teachings, she took a long sip of her martini then set the drink down before straightening her shoulders.

"Yes," Rowan said in her ear. "Be poised. A Dominant wants a submissive who will not crack. But tease him, be playful, and show him how much of a treat you are."

"Yeah. Yeah. Got it," she muttered. Alex had been around Hadley, Ryder's wife, enough that she simply mirrored her. Hadley was one of the strongest women Alex knew, but she explained once that she liked letting go at times and having Ryder take care of her. Cheaper than any therapy, Hadley once said.

Alex would rather pay for the therapy.

Once she had a plan in mind, she headed toward Lennox, who had yet to notice her. That had to change. When Alex reached the blond woman on his right, she bumped into the woman's arm and tossed her clutch purposely at Lennox's feet. Before anyone grabbed it, she dropped to her knees and scooped it up.

She gingerly looked up and said softly, "I'm so sorry, sir." She held his gaze as sensually as she could before she cast her eyes away. Okay, so this wasn't her thing, but she figured letting him hear the *sir*, while kneeling at his feet, would plant a good image in his mind.

A hand suddenly presented itself in front of her face. "Let me help you up."

*Gag!* This whole damsel-in-distress thing churned her stomach. "Oh, thank you so much." She slid her fingers into his hand, dragging them across his coarse skin, and *let* him help her to her feet. When she met his gaze again, she realized one very important fact. If Lennox was the killer, he needed to be taken out quickly. This guy had it all. Charisma, good looks, and money. A total triple threat that could lure women easily into his grip. She gave a shy smile. "I'm so clumsy sometimes. Again, I've very sorry."

Lennox returned the smile that oozed charm. "I'm just glad you're all right." He kept hold of her hand. "Heath Lennox." His chin dipped. "And you are?"

"Hadley Rose." Alex licked her lips, and his gaze flicked right there onto her mouth and held. The way his tongue sneaked out over his lips in response, she figured she was doing exactly what she should be doing.

"Walk away now," Rowan said in her ear.

Alex could have sworn she heard tension vibrating in his voice. She glanced down at their held hands and then purposely looked Lennox in the eye. She read romance novels. She knew the drill. She let her lips fall open, her breath catch, and she gave a slight shiver that only Lennox would notice because he held her hand. "Mr. Lennox," she said.

His gaze burned with heat and passion. "Ms. Rose."

Alex turned, and he slowly released her hand, but purposely dragged his index finger over her palm sensually. She strutted away, feeling his gaze following her every move, and put an extra wiggle to her hips.

"Is he watching me leave?" she asked Rowan.

"He's staring at your ass and drooling." A pause. "Now we just need to seal the deal."

Alex returned to the bar where she'd been standing before, keeping her back to Lennox. "Care to inform me how we do that?"

The air shifted, and the lust she lacked with Lennox suddenly engulfed her like wildfire as Rowan closed his hard body against her back. His lips grazed her neck, and a harsh shiver puckered her nipples when he murmured in her ear, "We make you a challenge."

# CHAPTER 7

EVERYTHING ALIGNED FOR Rowan when he brought Alex in close against him as they joined the other couples on the dance floor. This was where he wanted her, far away from Lennox. Right there next to him. Safe and close. Her spring-like scent infused the air around him, and there wasn't a single part of him that wanted to make her any more appealing to Lennox than she already was, but Mia's face filled his mind. Rowan held no doubt in his mind, Mia would know he was turning the world upside down trying to find her.

He brought Alex a little closer, all for the warmth she exuded. The slow sensual music filled the room. Rowan kept his hand low on Alex's back, not for Lennox, but all for himself. Touching her exactly like he wanted to touch her was his one indulgence tonight. Under different circumstances, Rowan would have allowed himself to drift away while he guided her along the dance floor, but tonight, he needed to stay sharp and ensure Alex caught Lennox's eye.

He dropped his head into her neck and inhaled her

aroma. A comforting scent that called to him on every level as a man. One he never seemed to get enough of, or never could have forgotten. And yet, he quickly pulled back, not letting his mind go where it wanted to linger.

With her mouth right by his ear, Alex asked, "You honestly think making me a challenge will grab Lennox's attention?"

Rowan pulled away to look down at her. "Yes."

Her expression pinched while she considered that. She finally snorted and shook her head. "Men are weird."

On that point, he would not argue with her. "Men like playing cat and mouse, especially if he is a Dominant. This would be intriguing for him. We're just hand-feeding Lennox that game."

She stopped dancing and scowled. "If I am the mouse in this scenario, I'm going to drop-kick you right here on the dance floor."

Rowan fought his smile, sliding his hand just a bit lower on her back, guiding her into the dance. "It's all acting, luv." When she didn't look convinced, he brought her in closer against his chest, feeling the swell of her breasts against him, drawn by how incredible and *right* she felt in his arms. That's what originally drew him to her when he met her in Paris. He'd never met anyone in his life that wasn't disposable, except for his family. Being a spy, he never got attached. But he hadn't liked the way Lennox looked at her, and he felt the surge of jealously burn through him.

Maybe his reaction was due to her strength. Or maybe it was because behind that ironclad wall she kept up, she had a good moral fiber that was unbreakable. Alex could work in the dark web and make millions, and yet she chose the path that took out the bad guys, one at a time. Rowan respected that, and her. But maybe, just *maybe,* his attachment was something else entirely. Something that he knew lingered deep in his chest that no woman had ever touched.

His cold, dead heart.

"I'm beginning to see the draw to this kind of work you do," Alex said, pulling him out of his thoughts. She gave him a sweet smile, one he didn't see very often. "You can be this rich partygoer one day, then someone totally different the next. It must be thrilling work."

"Beyond thrilling," he agreed.

From their week together in Paris, Rowan had learned that growing up had been hard for Alex. Her father was a deadbeat. Her mother was a drug addict who overdosed when Alex was sixteen years old. She'd been in and out of foster homes until she was an adult, but even Rowan knew she spent more time on the street than in any foster home.

Remembering all these details about Alex made him want to share part of himself with her too. "In my twenties, I lived for this type of life," he explained. "The adventure. The danger. It was the adrenaline rush I sought like an addict."

His emotions must have shown on his face. "And now, in your thirties, how is it?" she asked, a soft curl resting against the curve of her cheekbone.

He kissed that spot on her cheek, loving how she drew even closer toward him. "Now I see that this line of work comes at a price."

Her fingers tightened around his, head cocked and her eyes turning gorgeously inquisitive. "A price you don't want to pay anymore?"

He nearly answered, then stopped himself. After the Feds cut him out of the information loop, and the CIA wouldn't let him help, he started to question how much of himself he'd given up for the job, and since the minute he entered Alex's hotel room, he had started questioning life and what the hell he was doing with his. With Mia's life in danger, everything got put into perspective. Now... Christ, his mind definitely wasn't in the game. "The murder, the death, the darkness...it's grown exhausting. Add that to how the agency sidelined me on the case, I'm beginning to question my dedication to them." He let out the breath he'd unconsciously been holding. "There's gotta be something more to this world than seeing its dark underbelly."

Aware of it or not, she tightened the fingers clasped on his shoulder too. "That's why Ryder left the Army

Rangers. Too much death, and working in security has a lot fewer bad guys." She hesitated, obviously pondering something, and then her eyes filled with warm curiosity. "Have you ever considered the private sector? Ryder's always looking for new guys, especially former CIA."

He didn't hate the idea. A thought to consider later. He dipped his chin and held nothing back in his grin. "Are you asking me to move to San Francisco for you?"

Most women would blush and gasp or show some type of embarrassment. Alex held his gaze intently and smiled playfully back. "Believe me, Hawke, the last thing you'd want to do is move anywhere for me. I don't play nice."

He kept his mouth shut at that comment. Relationships couldn't have been an easy thing for her, not coming from the past she did. They weren't easy for him either. No wonder they'd both bolted five years ago.

Out of the corner of his eye, he watched Lennox leave his place next to his two trophy dates and move to the bar closest to them. Before Rowan could react to reel Lennox in, Alex's hand suddenly slid over his neck, bringing his focus back to her. When he met the swirling hints of brown within the amber hues of her eyes, he staggered to keep his mind steady, becoming so lost in their depths.

"Stop worrying," she said. "We're getting close to finding Mia. I can feel it."

She still thought Mia was on his mind. She was, of course, but Alex was there too. He stared intently, holding her close. He could never pinpoint the reason for the mess she created inside him when she watched him like he was her whole world for that moment, but all he knew was that she easily unraveled him. "Nothing is more dangerous to our task tonight than you looking at me like that," he told her seriously.

The side of her mouth curved. "And why is that?"

He dropped his mouth closer to hers and murmured, "For the control it has over me."

Her lips parted, inviting him to kiss her, whether she realized it or not. She pressed herself a little tighter against him, nearly making Rowan lose all sense of himself, but then he remembered why they were there. He drew in a deep breath to steady himself, and then leaned away, finding Lennox watching them. Rowan trailed his fingers gingerly up Alex's back and then down again, ensuring Lennox noticed how incredible she looked there all the way down to her smoking-hot ass. "How about you answer a question for me now?" Rowan asked, not only to keep their minds screwed on straight, but for his own curiosity.

She released a shuddering breath, obviously affected by the heat from his fingertips along her spine. "What do you want to know?"

"Why you were so agreeable to help me find Mia?"

The thought had been weighing on his mind since Alex had agreed back in the hotel room. He thought he'd need to lay claim to her physically to secure her to his side, but she barely hesitated to help once he told her the complete truth. "Not that I don't appreciate the help, but I saw the emotion in your face that day when I told you my sister was abducted; there's something driving you here, something personal."

She searched his eyes a moment then said, "I had a sister, and I understand that love."

"You *had* a sister?"

Alex gave a soft nod, glancing away for a moment before addressing him again. "Lena died when she was eighteen. I was seventeen."

Rowan tightened his fingers around Alex's hand, wanting to be anywhere but there while hearing such a personal conversation. "Do you mind explaining what happened to her?"

"What happens to the not-so-lucky foster kids," Alex said in a dry voice, lacking any emotion at all. "Lena had it rough, turned to drugs, and overdosed." Alex's expression couldn't lie, and pain waved off her. "We talked a lot even though we were placed in different foster homes after our mother passed away, but one night she went missing. I tried desperately to find her and then ended up racing around the city, looking in all the wrong places."

Every time Rowan learned more about Alex, he liked her a little bit more. She wasn't bitter, as he'd expected. She wasn't angry, as was warranted. She'd had a hard childhood but had come out on top of it. Something occurred to him then, making him curious. He stopped dancing, wanting to understand, and watched her intently. "Is that what got you into hacking?"

Alex gave a soft nod. "Had I had access to her cell phone, I could have saved her. I felt...*helpless*"—the word sounded strangled from her throat—"that night trying to find her. The police wouldn't help because it hadn't been twenty-four hours since she'd gone missing. When she eventually was found by tracking her cell phone, she had been dead for ten hours, alongside her boyfriend in a crack house, and I swore I'd never be that helpless again."

His fingers tightened possessively on her back. "And you haven't been."

"Never again," she said, holding his stare.

An emotion-packed beat passed between them.

No matter how hard Rowan tried to stay focused, he got caught up in her. And for one second, Rowan saw the side of Alex that he doubted most saw. The vulnerable side of her. The one that made Rowan only want to draw her closer, refusing to let go, no matter that he knew she didn't need him.

But that soft, emotional woman was quickly gone,

replaced by the hard woman determined to help him find Mia. "What's Lennox doing now?" she asked.

Rowan began dancing again, keeping Alex close. His stomach roiled at what she'd been through. He couldn't quite figure out how she'd come out of all that without bitterness and resentment, but damn, did she amaze him. He casually turned in their dance then caught sight of Lennox at the bar, his gaze burning with challenge and directed right at Rowan. "The cat caught the mouse."

"I really hate that metaphor," she muttered. "So, what now?"

Rowan began sliding his hand down her back sensually. "I'm going to grab your ass, and then you're going to slap me." He barely got a handful of her ass before she walloped him across the face, nearly making him see stars. His eyes began to water, and his cheek burned red-hot. "Fuck." He hadn't meant *that* hard.

"You pig!" Alex shouted in a fearful way that Rowan never would have thought she could pull off. "Security," she called, hugging herself. "Security."

Lennox was there in a second. "What's going on here?" he demanded, with his chest puffed out.

"He assaulted me!" Alex exclaimed, fake tears in her eyes as she inched her way closer to Lennox, playing the damsel-in-destress perfectly.

Damn, she'd make a fine CIA agent.

Security suddenly swarmed the area and had Rowan

by the arms. Everything went according to plan. Lennox swooped in to console Alex. Security was escorting Rowan out of the ballroom. But the one thing that Rowan hadn't been expecting was his reaction to watching Lennox wrapping an arm around Alex's shoulders and turning her away.

The fury that engulfed him was entirely unplanned. And so was the rage tightening his fists.

# CHAPTER 8

A LEX HAD TO give it to Rowan. His plan worked seamlessly. The security had swept Rowan out of the ballroom efficiently, and Lennox had taken Alex into the hotel's Presidential Suite.

"Just breathe." Rowan's voice was a smooth reassurance in her ear. "I'm close."

It occurred to her then that the earpiece must have had a GPS tracker too, considering how fast Rowan located her whereabouts.

The suite's door shut behind her, and as she followed Lennox into the two-story living room, she found panoramic views of the skyline through the floor-to-ceiling windows. In the corner of the suite was a baby grand piano, but Lennox moved in the other direction toward the small bar. The space was furnished with grand pieces and gold accents. Taking it all in, she moved to the double French doors, finding a wraparound balcony. Awestruck by the view, she exited the already-opened doors, greeted by a warm breeze.

"It's gorgeous, isn't it?"

Lennox's rumbly voice brushed against her ear. Alex purposely gasped a little, hoping he liked hearing her surprised by his nearness. She also reached into her clutch to take out the auto-injector before she turned around. He stood behind her, leaving very little room between them, and it crossed her mind that she might have placed herself directly in the line of a serial killer. "Everything about tonight has been incredible. You rescuing me from that handsy man, the ball, *this,* it's all so magical." *God, kill me now!* She swallowed back the bile in her throat.

He flashed her a charming smile then offered her a glass of whiskey on ice. "A little strong, but it'll take the edge off after dealing with that unpleasantness earlier."

She took the drink, not taking a sip, in case Lennox was their killer and he planned on drugging her. Keeping the auto-injector in her other hand, tucked behind her clutch, she said, "I really appreciate you stepping in for me like that." *Gag!* "I don't even know what came over that guy. All he wanted was a dance." Remembering to play her part, she averted her gaze, and said meekly, "I just…"

Lennox's finger came under her chin, and he brought her gaze back to his heated eyes. "…Should never have to deal with a man like that."

"You're right." She purposely breathed heavily. "No one should." And that, she actually meant.

Lennox slowly dragged his finger along her jawline. The oddness about it all was that under different circumstances, she'd probably be attracted to Lennox. She liked alpha guys. Sure, she was most definitely the wrong type of woman for him, but she couldn't help feeling a little flattered that this powerful billionaire seemed totally invested in her. Until she firmly reminded herself that he was also a possible killer. "You're a surprise I didn't intend for tonight," he finally said, releasing his hand to stuff it into his pocket.

"You're not the only one surprised," she said with a sweet smile.

He stayed exactly where he was, incredibly close, staring her down like she was some riddle he needed to solve. "You're not from around here?"

"How did you know that?" she asked playfully.

He dropped his gaze to her eye level. "Because I know everyone in *my* city, and you're not from my city."

She hesitated a moment, searching his eyes for any hint that he was about to push her off this balcony. "I'm actually from New York City," she said, moving around him and heading back into the living room, carefully keeping the auto-injector behind her clutch, not trusting that balcony anymore now that the thought had run through her mind.

"What do you do?" Lennox asked, following her inside.

"I'm in finance," she said, taking a seat on the piano's stool and crossing her legs on an angle to draw Lennox's attention.

It worked. His gaze ate up her legs. "You deal with money, then?"

"Mm-hmm," she purred, placing her untouched drink on the piano bench, and then she rose. She couldn't let this questioning continue. Heath Lennox had the brains along with the good looks. Too many questions would leave him suspecting something. Trying to remain playfully shy, she kept her eyes down when she approached him. "Is that why I'm here, though"—she stopped in front of him, slowly glancing up through her lashes—"to talk about my business?"

Alex met Lennox's smoldering eyes as he trailed a finger along her jawline. "Why do you want to be here?"

She licked her lips, drawing his attention to her mouth as she placed her clutch under her arm, keeping the auto-injector tucked in her palm. "I knew the second I saw you, I wanted you," she told him huskily, stepping a little closer, readying herself to stab his neck.

"Is that so?" He closed the distance between them, yanked her against him, and pressed his hefty erection against her thigh. Before she could act, he cupped her face and then he boldly kissed her.

Alex had kissed men like Lennox before. He kissed like he had the right to whatever he wanted and then he'd only demand more. And that was because he held the world at his fingertips. His kiss was meant to consume, yet it lacked that ravenous spark that Alex felt when Rowan placed his mouth on hers.

She began to lift her arm to inject the needle when a whistle came from behind her. Lennox broke the kiss in the same moment a fist flew by her face, and then a second later, Lennox staggered back, eventually landing on the ground, knocked out cold, blood trailing down his nose. Alex slowly turned around, finding Rowan standing behind her, fury etched into his face. "That was totally *not* in the plan." She sighed at him.

Rowan's gaze flicked to hers, his jaw muscles working. "An easier way of getting what we need?"

She snorted a laugh. "Oh, really?" They both knew that was total bullshit. "We gave our real names tonight. He's going to find out who I am. He's a smart guy."

Rowan glared at Lennox. "I'm sure you'll come up with something." He pressed his lips shut, but the tightness around his eyes gave him away. He was 100 percent jealous. And since Alex hadn't had anyone be jealous over her in longer than she cared to admit, she found it sort of endearing.

Endearing if it didn't come from a CIA agent who always had an agenda, of course.

She quickly moved to Lennox then flipped him over and lifted his shirt. "Damn." No tattoo.

"Fuck," Rowan said, thrusting his fingers into his hair in frustration.

Alex dropped Lennox's shirt, wanting to move to Rowan, feeling heartbroken for him. All these dead ends couldn't be easy. But as soon as she went to move, Lennox began groaning. Alex stuck him with the auto-injector to give them time to get out.

"Let's go," she said, pulling on Rowan's arm to get him moving.

They dodged the security waiting at the end of the hallway and made it to the staircase. The only sound while they descended the staircase was Alex's high heels on the cement floor.

Only when they were back in the limo that was already waiting outside did she turn and look at Rowan. He sat next to her with his head resting back against the headrest, eyes closed. His chest rose and fell quickly from their run down the stairs, but it was his stillness that she noted most.

"Where to?" the limo driver asked.

Alex rambled off the address for the airport, unable to take her eyes off Rowan. She reached for his hand. "We're going to find her."

She saw his deep swallow and understood it too. The FBI couldn't find this killer. She didn't have any success so far either. And she had felt this pain. She knew what it was like to have someone you loved missing. It hurt with every breath.

He finally exhaled deeply then turned his head and looked at her, and there was a vulnerability she'd never seen in him before. "Time is against us," he told her with a tight voice. "Mia is waiting for me to find her."

Alex paused, wanting to find the right thing to say. She decided on: "Why do you think I'm brought in on difficult cases?"

"Because you're the best," he said immediately.

She slowly shook her head, taking one of his hands in both of hers. "Because I never stop trying, not since my sister." She leaned just a little closer, drawing in Rowan's scent instead of Lennox's. "I know what's on the line. That's what drives me. So no one ever has to feel what I felt when Lena died. I *will* find Mia."

Rowan's expression softened, and he cupped Alex's face. His eyes searched hers while the shadows passed over his face as they drove beneath the streetlights, and then his lips met hers. She felt the raw emotion in his kiss, the sense of urgency in his quivering muscles, and she felt helpless too.

He eventually broke the kiss and leaned his forehead against hers. "You were right, you know."

"Right about what?" she asked, moving away to hold his intense stare.

He brushed his thumb across her bottom lip then arched an eyebrow. "I did not like seeing his lips on yours." A thousand things passed in the air between them. Things that were so easy and yet so damn complicated at the same time. "And when this is all over and we have Mia home, we're going to talk more about that. Really talk without the two of us bailing on that conversation."

Alex didn't have the words she needed, so she simply nodded then glanced out her window, watching the busy streets pass her by, realizing this was the first time she'd actually considered having that talk, instead of running.

# CHAPTER 9

O N THE FLIGHT back to New York City, Alex had
kept her nose stuck in her laptop. Rowan had
stayed quiet, trying desperately to control his frustration.
Every step forward only seemed to get him that much
further away from finding Mia. His parents were on his
mind. Christ, he did not want to make that call. And yet,
as much as that consumed him, so did the thought of
Mia and the life that she should have.

Doubt and sadness continued to engulf him when
they landed then took the limo back to the hotel. That
dread and worry rested heavy in his chest while he left
Alex in the living room and showered. The hot water
beat at his tense muscles, and he let the heat take him
away from there for a moment.

By the time he finished his shower and redressed in
fresh clothes, he rinsed all the bad shit away and
refocused his attention. They needed to find Mia,
nothing else was acceptable. And Alex would find her.

Rowan held onto his belief in that.

When he reentered the living room, he leaned against

the doorframe between the bedroom and the living room. The lamp on the side table was turned on, casting a warm glow into the space. Alex sat in the big chair with her legs pulled up beneath her while she typed away on her laptop. She was gorgeous. So focused on the task, she didn't even realize he entered the room. He couldn't look away, so lost in *her*.

*How am I going to let you go this time?*

The thought nearly crippled him. She'd go back to San Francisco again. He believed that as much as he believed they'd find Mia alive. But he wasn't the same man who'd run from her in Paris. His perspective had changed. His wants for his life all looked very different now. In the end, did he want to be remembered as CIA Agent Rowan Hawke, or something more?

He wasn't sure.

"You're staring." Alex's soft voice broke into his thoughts. He blinked, finding her curious gaze on him before returning to her screen. "Everything all right?"

Nothing was all right, but he didn't want to make this situation any more complicated than it already was. At least, not yet. "I need a job to do while you're doing yours." He couldn't stand the silence anymore. The waiting. The worrying.

She didn't take her eyes off the monitor, like she hadn't even heard him, so tuned into her work. "I've missed something. I can feel it. There's gotta be someone else who's here. There's just no way it's not about this app."

Rowan understood those type of instincts to stay focused and get the job done. He had them himself. He also knew if he felt like he was onto something, nothing would tear him away. "I'm sure you're right, Alex, but what can I do to help you?"

Maybe it was the tightness in his voice or the near desperation to be of any assistance at all, but she finally lifted her head again. The makeup under her eyes was smudged, but even so, he could still see dark circles there too. Part of him felt like a selfish prick for bringing her into this, knowing emotionally if they didn't find his sister, Alex would take it as a hit too. The other part of him knew he had no chance of finding Mia without her.

Alex searched his eyes with a soft look of understanding, then said, "Caffeine and food would be great."

He doubted she was hungry. She was just throwing him a bone, and for that, he was grateful. "Any food in particular?" he asked.

"Something with substance."

He nodded. "That I can do. I'll be back soon."

She barely gave him another second of her focus before she turned her full attention to her monitor and her fingers began flying across her keyboard. Rowan moved to the door and slipped on his boots, then gave her a final look before leaving. He'd have to find a way to repay Alex, though he wasn't sure how he could ever repay her if they found Mia.

Or maybe he'd let Mia show her gratitude. His baby sister had a way with people that Rowan never did.

Once in the hallway, he took the stairs instead of the elevator, trotting down the sixteen floors. When he made it out into the late, chilly night, Mia's talks with him filled his memory. He'd thought a thousand times over of all the conversations they'd had recently, looking for anything that would bring him closer to this killer. But there was nothing else there. Nothing his sweet, lively sister told him that would help. Not once had Rowan allowed himself to think about what his sister might be going through. The only thought he had was finding her, and fuck, he felt like he was failing her.

Though as he passed beneath the streetlight, with the slight fog in the air tonight, he hoped wherever Mia was, she knew he wouldn't stop searching. His sister was strong and fierce, much like Alex, only a little softer and sweeter, definitely more sheltered, and she was smart. She'd stay alive.

He headed down the street, searching out anything he thought Alex might like. He passed a tavern and quite a few five-star restaurants that were long closed for the night, until he noticed a shawarma place up ahead on the right.

A laughing couple passed him on the street before he

entered the small restaurant with red metal tables on one side and a long counter on the other with a cash register at the end of the counter.

Rowan quickly moved there, passing three people sitting at a table near the glowing open sign on the window. "Two beef shawarmas and a couple of Cokes," he said to the female cashier, grabbing his wallet.

"That'll be twenty-two dollars," she said, after hitting the buttons on the register.

He paid his bill then moved to the other side of the long counter, waiting for his number to be called while the female clerk tended to the next customer.

The television screen was on up in the corner of the restaurant, not playing a sports game as one would expect. The station was airing the rerun of the press conference held a day ago with the Director of the FBI, Carl Lewis. In his early fifties, Lewis was clean-cut, clean-shaven, and in good shape. His round blue eyes held wisdom and strength, and he wore a suit as well as any businessman on Wall Street. The man had been in the media more than out of it lately. The face of the investigation that was going nowhere, yet he seemed to excel in manipulating the media to believe otherwise.

"At this time, are there any new developments in locating the Casanova Sadist?" a reporter called from the audience.

"Every day there are new developments," Lewis said

calmly. "We're working every angle, twenty-four seven."

"Bullshit," Rowan muttered to himself. He'd seen the FBI files. They had no angle, no evidence, nothing.

Another reporter called out, "Do you have any new suspects?"

"I cannot discuss that at this time, as I don't want to hinder the investigation." Lewis pointed to another reporter. "Yes."

"Should the city go on a lockdown?"

Carl's blue eyes warmed and he held up a hand. "I know the people of New York City are afraid, but I assure you, everyone is safe. Yes, take extra caution. Be wise. But the FBI is working diligently on this case. We will not rest until we get the women home and arrest whoever is responsible for these heinous crimes."

The front door of the store suddenly flew open, jolting Rowan into awareness. He relaxed when a group of teenagers came inside and hurried to three other teenagers sitting at a table.

Rowan only caught pieces of what the kid said. "Dude...hotel...fire...come on."

A hot rush of unease crept over Rowan. His instincts had saved his life many times, but they also warned him of danger just as much. He stepped closer to the group. "Hey, kid."

The blue-haired teenager turned around, chest heaving with the obvious exertion of running there. "Yeah?"

"What hotel was on fire?"

"Landon—"

Rowan didn't even let the kid finish. He bolted toward the door. Hotel fires were few and far between, but pulling an alarm was also the easiest way to clear a hotel when a killer needed, and wanted, possible witnesses cleared. Rowan had done it himself, many times.

"Sir," the server called as he threw the door open. "Your food!"

Rowan didn't look back. He ran. To Alex.

# CHAPTER 10

THE FIRE ALARM blaring out in the hallway had Alex shutting her laptop to go and investigate. She moved to the front door, not minding the interruption. No matter how many scripts she ran, she still got nowhere, except for hitting one server that whoever was on the other end had knowledge of how to keep her out. That server had been the one she'd been working on for the last hour. Usually if someone wanted to keep a hacker like her out, there was good reason.

When she opened the door, she found the guests leaving their rooms and moving to the staircase. *Great.* She hurried back to grab her laptop and then slipped into her shoes before heading for the door again. The heavy door opened a mere crack before it was slammed open, sending both Alex and her laptop crashing to the floor.

There was no chance to look up and see what happened or who stood there. There were only fingers tight on her neck and a heavy body crushing down on her. She barely got her eyes open enough to see a face, one she didn't recognize, but she stared into the piercing brown eyes in the seconds before she caught his arm, pushing hard against it to stop the gun from aiming at her head.

*Rowan.*

Seconds felt like a minutes-long moment in hell as she realized someone was there to kill her. And thus came the realization that whoever's server she hit knew exactly who she was and where she was staying.

Her heart rate thundered in her ears. The scream desperate to rip from her throat in a call for help was right there, but died when his fingers tightened more and more, while his knee dug into her chest. Blackness began to creep into her vision, and she knew that would be the end of her. And yet...*and yet,* there was no moving him off, no getting away. She thrashed beneath him, but her hand on his gun was the only thing keeping her from dying right there on the hotel floor.

*Rowan.*

Then her arms weakened, the strain far too much for her to hold. The gun, with a silencer, slowly began to turn closer to her face, her arms shaking.

*This is it...*

*Rowan...*

A sudden loud bang followed by another bang that was deafening and echoed in the suite eased the darkness slightly. And then there was only a dead weight onto her chest, pressing against her with unbearable heaviness.

Until that weight was gone.

"Jesus Christ," Rowan growled, reaching for Alex. "Where are you bleeding?" he asked calmly, even if his gaze suggested he wasn't calm at all.

Alex, finally coming to her senses, glanced down, finding her hands and the rest of her body covered in blood. "No. No." She gasped. "It's not my blood."

"Some of it is," he said, then tilted her head to the side and looked at her neck. "He must be wearing a ring. He caught you here. You'll need a few stitches."

The pain didn't even register. Nothing registered until Rowan cupped her face.

"Are you okay?" he asked.

She nodded, and then nodded again, actually believing it this time. But then she was struck by the realization that the only person who crossed her mind in those seconds she thought her life was over was Rowan. Not Ryder, her closest friend and the only person she trusted. Just Rowan. Not even able to grasp what that meant, she glanced at the deceased man. "Oh, no, Rowan, what have you done?" It occurred to her then that any chance they had at finding Mia was gone. Rowan had just killed the Casanova Sadist.

Rowan slowly rose, as if letting her go pained him. Right now, she didn't want him to let her go either. She realized she shook from her head to toe, the scary awareness suddenly dawning on her that she'd nearly been murdered, if Rowan hadn't gotten there in time.

He moved to the man, then lifted up the man's shirt. "I doubt this is our killer. It's not his style." He shoved the man over. After which, he reached for his cell phone and took a picture of his face. "But I'm going to find out who he is and get this cleaned up."

"We can use Ryder," Alex said, rubbing her neck and pushing her shaky self off the ground to get farther away from the dead man. He was on the floor, bleeding all over the carpet with a gunshot wound in his chest and in his head.

"There's no need," Rowan said. He dialed a phone number then pressed the phone to his ear. "I need a cleanup at the Landon Bridge hotel room number 1602."

"How are you going to explain *this*"—she pointed at the dead guy—"to the CIA? You're not working a case."

"I'm always working a case," Rowan responded. "I'm just not supposed to be working my sister's case." He moved back to the man and grabbed the guy's wallet from his back pocket. He took a look at his ID. "Jimmy Valens." Rowan's eyes flicked to Alex, concern heavy in their depths. "Do you know him?"

She shook her head, aware of the warm blood dripping off her hands, and now feeling her own blood trickling down her neck. Her stomach roiled, so she went back to her earlier thought. "What do you mean, you don't need to explain to the CIA when you kill a man?"

Rowan shot her a measured look. "In my line of work, causalities are part of the business. Besides, Valens has given us a way to dispose of him."

Brows up, and fighting against the sickness turning her stomach inside out, Alex asked, "How?"

"The fire."

She turned to the deceased man. He was looking right at her. She swallowed her emotions. Death was never anything she'd been good at handling. Exactly why her job never happened on site.

"What do you have?"

She glanced up as Rowan spoke again, but not to her. She found him on his cell phone. "Yeah," he said. "All right. Yes, I'm leaving now." He ended the call then looked at Alex. "Gather your things. We need to go." He headed into the closet and took all her clothes out, including the hangers. He tossed a new shirt at her and she quickly changed and handed Rowan her soiled shirt. "Go wash your hands and face. Put a cloth on that wound."

Her body felt light, her mind not really there when she entered the bathroom. She saw the darkness in her eyes, the absent, mindless look in them too, when she began washing her hands and face. Rowan wasn't wrong—the cut on her neck was deep, gaping open, and definitely needed stitches. She hurried to get herself cleaned up then grabbed the washcloth off the towel rack, placing that against her neck to stop the bleeding. She finished up by throwing all her makeup into her night bag then left the bathroom.

Rowan stood over the dead body with a frown.

"Regretting shooting him now?" she asked, closing in on him. Ryder always preferred to keep people alive to question them.

"He almost killed you," Rowan said, slowly lifting his eyes to hers. They were tense. "I will never regret killing him."

She saw the intensity in his gaze. The warm affection and the sweet worry there too. And without thought, she moved closer to him, needing his warmth, needing him to get this chill out of her blood.

When she reached him, he wrapped her in his arms, holding her close. She shut her eyes, falling into his warm embrace, as he added, "Besides, he's a hired hitman on the FBI's Most Wanted List."

She let out a long, deep breath at that. Killing anyone was wrong, but at least this guy wouldn't take any more innocent lives than he'd already had.

Before she could voice her thoughts, Rowan leaned away then dropped his eyes level with hers. "We can't linger here. Are you okay to leave?"

She nodded quickly, still feeling her limbs shaking.

He released her to grab her suitcase. Alex moved to

the wall to take out her laptop charger next to the chair then followed Rowan out. He took her hand, and they hurried into the hallway. She kept the washcloth tight against her neck as they passed firemen in the stairwell yelling at them to get out.

Rowan stayed silent, and she could see his training now. He was stealthy and methodical in the way he moved. Really, in how he dealt with the entire situation. And it wasn't until Rowan had her out on the street and a block away from the hotel that he turned and looked deeply at her. He cupped her face and closed in on her until her back was pressed against the brick wall of the store behind her. He stared intently. Warmly, even. "I have only been afraid like that once before now. And that was when I heard Mia had been abducted."

Her breath caught at the emotion in his eyes, and sudden unexpected tears rose that Alex could do nothing to stop. Her heart squeezed in his warm protection, and for right now, she wasn't thinking of all the complications between them. Her heart wanted this guy holding her close. "You got there in time."

"Always." His voice was thick with similar emotion, his tormented gaze saying so much. He sealed his mouth against hers in a fierce kiss, and she tumbled into all that Rowan offered her.

But most of all, she let herself be vulnerable and leaned on him when everything in this moment seemed dangerous.

When he eventually broke the kiss, he stated, "I will always get there in time, Alex. *Always.* Tell me you believe me."

A tear she couldn't stop leaked from her eye, and as he wiped it away, she whispered, "I believe you."

# CHAPTER 11

I N CHINATOWN, AFTER Rowan placed a quick call to an old friend, he entered the four-digit code onto the keypad and opened the back door of the small doctor's office. Once Alex scooted in, he locked the door behind them, purposely not turning on the lights as he headed down the hallway and entered the first examination room. He grabbed the gooseneck exam lamp and flicked the light on, illuminating a room with cartoon drawings covering the walls. He glanced Alex's way, finding her examining the space with clear confusion. He fought his smile and smacked the examination table. "Up you get."

She set those inquisitive eyes on him before she moved to the table and hopped up, her legs dangling off the side. "Whose office is this?"

"A friend," Rowan answered. He avoided her gaze and *that* topic, then he left the exam room to enter the room next door and grabbed a suture tray that was in the exact place it'd been the last time Rowan visited this office a year ago. Nothing in the office had changed.

When he returned to Alex, he found her smiling,

even though she had the washcloth pressed against her neck and she had to feel some pain. It also didn't surprise him when she said, "Not just a friend, an ex-girlfriend, I take it."

Alex didn't miss much. He liked that about her too.

Rowan nodded, placing the suture tray next to her on the examination table. "Her name is Abigail. We dated for a short time ten years ago, but now, we're just good friends." He wheeled the light closer. "A friend who lets me use her place for situations like this. A friend who is happily married now with two children," he added, in case she had the same jealous streak that he appeared to hold when it came to her.

"Without any questions asked?" Alex asked.

He unwrapped the tray then grabbed two latex gloves from the box on the wall. When he slipped his hand into one, he answered, "Like I said, she's a good friend." He wiggled his hand into the second glove then reached for the needle and the local anesthetic.

When he lifted both, Alex cleared her throat. "Not that I doubt you here, but how many times have you stitched someone up?"

"Enough to know what I'm doing," he answered, sliding the needle into the medicine bottle and pulling back on the handle to draw in the medicine. He flicked the needle, getting rid of the air bubbles then placed it back down on the tray. "Here, let me have a look first."

Alex cringed when she pulled away the cloth. The bleeding had stopped, but the small wound gaped open. He pressed against the sides, making sure nothing was lodged in the wound, but he couldn't find anything there.

He noted the way she held her breath and the tightness in her jaw. "You don't have to put on a brave face for me, luv. I know this hurts, believe me."

She gave a tight laugh and a loud snort. "Hurry up and stab me with the needle, will ya?"

He proceeded to do just that. When he finished up with the anesthetic, ensuring she'd be completely numb soon, she let out the breath she'd been holding. He gave a soft smile. "Let's give that a few minutes to kick in."

She held his gaze. "Were you and Abigail serious?"

He set the needle back on the tray then turned to her, examining the intrigue in her gaze. Were they taking a step forward? Alex rarely asked about his past. He thought that was mostly because she didn't want to remember hers, so she stayed in the present. "We were about as serious as I've ever gotten with a woman." He gave a small smile. "Until we weren't, of course."

"Was that her decision or yours?"

"Hers," he explained, ensuring not to touch anything to keep his gloves uncontaminated. "It's hard to have a relationship with someone who isn't there, both physically and mentally."

Alex smiled. "The CIA gig, huh?"

He nodded. "The job back then was all-consuming. Abigail deserved better. She knew that, and so did I." He reached for the needle again then used the sharp end to poke at the open wound. "Feel that?"

"Nope."

The tension in his chest lightened some. "Good." He took the gauze from the tray and dosed it in iodine before he gently began to wipe at the wound. When she didn't flinch, he pressed a little harder, making sure he got anything in there out, to avoid infection. "And what about you?" he asked.

Her brows rose. "What about me?"

He tossed the gauze back on the tray then opened the sealed package containing the suture needle and blue thread. Using the tissue forceps, he picked up the needle with the needle driver and began his first stitch. "Any serious relationships?"

She snorted a laugh. "Serious relationships happen when you trust people. I don't trust anyone but Ryder."

At that comment, he looked her right in the eye. She trusted him to a point, and they both knew it. "Professional hazard?"

She shrugged. "Something like that."

Most times, he'd let her dodge him. For some reason, tonight, he couldn't. "Explain that."

"What's to explain?" she asked. "I don't do serious."

He knew why—her past. He also didn't feel the need to question her about that either. He understood her hang-ups. "A personal hazard, then?"

She gave a small smile and repeated, "Something like that too."

Yeah, he got it, all right. Hard to want or trust a relationship when the only relationships you saw were held together with drugs and alcohol and abuse. Though as they stayed silent while he finished the four stitches then tied the knot and cut the remaining thread, he wondered if he could change her mind about that.

When he placed the scissors back on the tray, her hand came down on his arm, and her voice softened. "It was complicated."

His gaze flicked to hers. "What was complicated?"

"Paris." A beat passed between them, her eyes searching his. Until she finally spoke again. "We couldn't have made it work. So many things stood in our way. Things that were unchangeable."

He swallowed the tightness back in his throat, letting him breathe easier. Then he spoke the words on his mind since he realized again how great she was, and how incredible they were together. "Yeah, it was complicated then. Now I'm not sure it is."

"I don't—"

"You *do* trust me," he interjected.

Emotion rose in her expression, softening Alex in

ways Rowan had never seen. Her brows drew together and her lips parted, but a beep cut off whatever she was planning to say. She reached into her back pocket and drew out her phone.

In an instant, Rowan saw the color drain from her face. "What is it?"

She slowly glanced up, meeting his gaze. "Ryder wanted to give us a heads-up. Another body has been found."

The room spun slightly before Rowan gripped the exam table, pressing his feet hard against the floor to ground himself. He knew it should register that apparently Ryder was working the case now, but nothing mattered beyond the dark thoughts racing through Rowan's mind. He shut his eyes and breathed deep before meeting Alex's gaze again. "Is it Mia?"

Her fingers tightened around his arms. "Ryder doesn't know."

Rowan dropped his head, controlling the rage, sadness, and fear that invaded every crevice of his mind.

"I'm so sorry, Rowan," Alex whispered.

He lifted his head, staring deeply at the woman he never could forget. "You know this pain."

Her eyes saddened. "I do." She cupped his face. "Ryder can get us any information we need."

"We don't need him," Rowan said, moving away to quickly but efficiently clean the wound then put a bandage over top.

"How, then?"

He tossed the tray in the garbage can before taking Alex's hand. "I'll get us on the scene."

# CHAPTER 12

A QUARTER OF an hour later, Alex waited by the side of the road, next to a farmer's hayfield. The dark night surrounded her, minus the numerous cop cars with their lights flashing and the spotlights beaming down on the roped-off crime scene out in the famer's field. Rowan stood just outside the yellow tape with a lanky, tall man with dark brown hair and even darker eyes that hadn't showed much emotion when she'd met him a handful of minutes ago before her nonstop ringing cell phone had her turning away from them.

That was two minutes ago. For those last minutes, Ryder had been drilling her. "For the last time," Alex said into her phone, "I. Am. Fine. Please stop worrying about me."

"You were attacked and hurt, and someone tried to kill you," Ryder snapped. "How can I not worry?"

"You sure know a lot for someone who is not sup-posed to be having me watched," she grumbled back at him.

"Alex," he warned.

She ignored his snippy voice, knowing having Ryder there would only cause more tension, considering even she realized the stakes now. The killer knew who she was, and apparently, had hired Valens to take her out. Which, of course, only told her she was looking in the right place. Something she'd get back to just as soon as could. "Did you run Valens?" she asked, refocusing on what mattered—finding this bastard. "Get anything on him?"

"He's a hired thug that's on the FBI's Most Wanted List," Ryder reported "Rich. Obviously good at his job."

"Well, not good enough, since I'm not dead," she pointed out.

"Without Hawke, that would not be the case." It was a rare thing for Ryder to sound impressed over anyone, unless they were a member of his team. "Run that name by me again, the guy who you're with now."

"Wes Lanning," she said, glancing toward Rowan and Wes who were still standing by the yellow tape. "He's an old military buddy of Rowan's. FBI." And Wes was the *only* reason they were allowed there.

"All right," Ryder said. "You're at the location of the murder now?"

"Yup, just waiting to view the body," she said, noting the tension along Rowan's shoulders, even though he kept his hands stuffed in his pockets, obviously trying to portray calmness in a moment he couldn't have been calm at all.

Ryder hesitated for longer than necessary, and when he spoke again, some of the tightness had left his voice. "Dare I ask why Rowan needs to identify the body?"

Alex fought against the roll of her stomach. She'd wondered the same thing and asked that very question when they had arrived. She hadn't liked the answer she got. "The head is gone."

"The woman's head?"

Alex groaned, pressing her hand against her stomach. "Please don't make me say it again."

Ryder *harrumphed,* paused, then said sternly, "I'm coming there."

"You'd have nothing to do," Alex countered gently. Of course, she appreciated Ryder wanting to keep her safe, but the last thing she wanted was to get Ryder dragged into all this. "I'm closing in on this guy. Tonight's event is proof of that. We'll get somewhere safe after this…and honestly, if the victim is Mia…" She couldn't even finish, hoping with everything in her that it wasn't.

"If it's Mia, you'll come home, and let the FBI and CIA handle this, right?" Ryder finished for her.

The question hung in the dark night. Which was…*odd.* Of course, Alex was going back to San Francisco…*right?*

As if he knew where her thoughts lingered, Rowan turned around, his intense gaze boring deeply into hers.

He finally waved her over.

"Listen, I gotta go," she said to Ryder.

"You never answered my question," Ryder grumbled.

"Talk soon." She ended the call immediately, not ready to answer the question. Not even understanding *why* she couldn't answer that question. She tucked her phone into the back pocket of her jeans then hurried to Rowan's side. "It's time?"

Rowan nodded.

Wes interjected and said to her firmly, "Put your hands in your pockets and do not take them out."

Alex blinked at him. "Seriously?"

"Seriously." Wes nodded. "Hawke shouldn't be here. The only reason he is here is because I got clearance for him to identify the body. You absolutely have no reason to be here. Do not fuck with my crime scene."

She'd met hard-asses over the years. Hell, she worked for Ryder, and he was the king of being a hard-ass. But she got the feeling that Wes was not a man to push around, and knowing she was there for Rowan, and Mia, she shut her usually loud mouth and shoved her hands into her pockets.

"Good," Wes said, giving her an approving nod. To Rowan, he said, "I'll say it again: Are you sure you're ready for this? It's…" His lips pinched in a firm line before he continued. "This isn't a good scene."

Rowan didn't even hesitate. "I need to know. Let's

go."

Wes's shoulders rose and fell with his heavy breath, then he glanced at Alex. "Not a step out of place."

He raised the yellow tape, and she followed Rowan beneath. Suddenly Rowan turned back and grabbed her arm. "You don't need to see this."

"Yeah, well, you're not seeing this without me." Even though there was a trepidation running beneath the surface of her strength, she pulled away from his hand and followed Wes toward all the bright lights. She felt Rowan follow.

She'd never seen her sister's dead body, but she would have given anything to have had Rowan with her when she found out Lena was dead.

The closer they got, the more she realized the body lay near a small forested area. First, she saw a foot, then a whole leg, all the way up to the naked torso. The killer hadn't even tried to hide the body. He had placed her on full display, like some sick piece of artwork. Which, as Alex moved closer, she admitted to herself made the scene slightly easier to take in.

She found very little blood. The body lay in a position that looked very similar to a move a ballet dancer would make. And in the place of the woman's head was a bouquet of roses. So many things rushed through her mind, ready to fall out of her mouth, but she kept her lips pressed shut, knowing no matter how disturbing this was to her, it had to be much worse for Rowan.

With her heart in her throat, disregarding Wes's order, she took her hands out of her pockets and reached out to find Rowan's hand. He gripped her fingers tight and stepped closer. When she moved in next to him, she gave him a quick look and was surprised to find that his gaze was not shocked or disturbed, but focused, searching the body.

"Is it Mia?" Wes asked, sidling up to them.

Rowan finally let out his breath. "I don't know. Can I get closer?"

Wes nodded. "You can, but don't touch."

Rowan gave Alex's hand a final hard squeeze then approached the woman. Standing on top of the pressed-down hay, he scanned every inch of her skin, until he settled on her right hip. "Mia had a chicken pox scar on her hip here. I'm not seeing it." He glanced over his shoulder at Alex. "You?"

It occurred to her that it was the worst time for her to feel flattered that he looked to her, not his good friend Wes, but she appreciated that he valued her input. She leaned in a little closer. "I don't see a scar."

Relief and emotions that Alex couldn't put a name to even if she tried, rushed across Rowan's expression. He turned back to the woman, and if Alex hadn't been listening closely, she would have missed when he said, "I'm sorry, sweet girl." With his hard expression back in place, he said to Wes, "Thank you for arranging this. If anything else comes up, you'll let me know?"

"Of course." Wes stepped forward and cupped Rowan's shoulder. "I won't stop trying to find her."

"I know." Rowan gave a firm nod then glanced at Alex. "We'll keep you in the loop on our end."

Wes inclined his head, then he turned away and moved toward the cops waiting at their vehicles.

Alex felt the slight tremble in Rowan's hand when he slid his fingers in hers and led her away from the scene toward the Uber that waited for them on the side of the road.

Once the bright lights of the crime scene began to fade, she pulled a little against his hand. "Just wait a second."

He glanced down at her, then, and the glow of the lights behind him displayed the dark pain in his eyes, and she knew exactly what he needed right now.

It wasn't to talk.

She slid her arms around his middle, offering him the warmth she'd needed when Lena had first gone missing. He stayed tense for a long moment before he finally sighed, his arms wrapping around her while his lips came down on the top of her head.

# CHAPTER 13

ONLY A FEW blocks away from Central Park, Rowan brought Alex back to his one-bedroom apartment. Alex went straight for the leather couch against the far wall between the two windows and set her laptop against the armrest of the couch, curling her legs up underneath her. "I need more time with that one server," she said.

What she probably needed was sleep, but Rowan knew that wouldn't happen for either of them anytime soon. "I'm going to shower," he said.

She didn't even look up. "Mmm."

Exhaustion weighed him down as he moved toward the bathroom. There, he wasted no time shedding his clothes and then getting into the shower, turning the water onto hot. He'd felt conflicted many times in his life. Over many different things. But the feeling of relief that hit him when he didn't see Mia's chicken pox scar left him feeling sick to his stomach. He'd so desperately wanted it to be another woman, and yet when he saw that poor woman left in the way the killer had left her, he felt sickened that he'd prayed it hadn't been Mia.

Beneath the hot stream of water, he dropped his head, allowing the water to beat against his hard muscles.

*Mia.*

His sister was a fighter. She was the little girl on the playground who beat up the boy bullies. She was strong and loyal and all the good that was in this world. And he wanted her close. Safe.

Yet, every step he took forward only seemed to place him farther away. Tonight, seeing the victim there reminded Rowan of the stakes here. If he didn't find Mia and *soon*, that would be her body in the next field.

He couldn't let that happen. The thoughts of his mother falling to her knees, brokenhearted, and of his father, torn apart by grief, nearly sent him to his knees. His parents needed him to find her. Mia needed him to find her. He couldn't fail them.

Rowan had no idea how much time had passed when the sudden click of the shower door caught his attention. He glanced back, finding Alex standing there, fully clothed. Every raw emotion burning within suddenly amplified. She felt like the one piece that kept him together in all this. As long as she was there, he knew they had a fighting chance. And the more time he spent with her, the more he knew that having her support meant more to him than having her hacking skills. He needed her there. He wanted her there. He felt less unraveled with her.

Her lips parted as she took in a harsh breath. "I've got—"

He let everything he wanted and needed flood into him in this moment and yanked her inside the shower. She squealed as he pulled her tight against him, into the stream of the water. Her eyes widened at whatever showed on his expression. He was sure it was a mix of dark pain and hot desire.

She blinked once and then said, "—some news."

He scanned over her lips—that mouth that made him hungry. He glanced down at her breasts beneath her wet shirt, feasting upon her hard nipples. Then he drew her closer, pressing her up against his hard cock.

She slid her hands up his arms, his muscles quivering beneath her touch. "I haven't found Mia yet, but you'll want to hear what I have to say."

"I need you," he said, loudly and firmly, and she shut her mouth. "I'm a step away from losing the very things that hold me together." He reached for the hem of her shirt and had it over her head faster than he was sure she expected. "And you're the thing keeping me from losing it." He knew what he was throwing out into the world with that statement. He didn't care either.

Tonight, at that scene in the farmer's field, he knew life was too fucking short. In a blink of an eye, everything could change. Five years ago, Alex had left an impression on him that he couldn't forget. Now she had taken his heart and he didn't want it back. He knew the day he met her the danger she presented to him. She'd shown him another side of life. And being with her again made him understand he wanted that life.

He was done running.

When she stayed silent and stared at him wide-eyed, he added, "I've spent my life doing the right thing. And in the end, the sweetest, most innocent person I know is in the hands of a fucking cruel killer."

Heady emotion crossed Alex's expression while she cupped his face. "Don't fall apart on me now. We're going to find her."

"You can't promise that," he said. "No one can. All that's left in this world is evil fucking people and the terrible shit they do. But then there is you…" Her fingers tightened, her breath hitching a little, as he continued. "You're one good thing in this fucked-up world. I'm done not saying it. You came back into my life exactly when I needed you. That's twice now." Her bra followed before he unflicked the button on her jeans and then yanked those down until she was stepping out of them.

When he straightened up, she said, "I know you're feeling emotional, but I think you're going to want to—"

He grasped her hip then turned her until her back pressed against the tile on the wall. "No more talking," he growled against her mouth. He didn't wait for a reply.

He crushed his mouth against hers, and he felt the tremble of her body when she relaxed and melted beneath his touch.

He kissed her roughly, passionately, not letting her for one second avoid following where he wanted them both to go. He wanted her. No, *needed* her. To feel anything but this horrible awareness that he was one step away from losing the sweet, innocent sister he adored and having to crush his parents' hearts.

Alex gave him that safe place. Christ, she *was* the safe place where he could let everything go and know that somehow, he could lay all of his heavy shit on her and she could support it, and him, until he could make his way back to himself.

The water rained down on them as he reached for her thigh and hooked it over his hip. He gave her direct eye contact. "Are you protected?"

She nodded and gasped, wiggling against him. "Yes. IUD." Then she reached around and grasped his ass in her hands, moving him closer.

He entered her with a hard thrust forward, sending her up on her tiptoes, and he went cross-eyed. Her hot and wet heat surrounded him, and he'd never felt anything so incredible in his life. She moaned against his mouth, and he kissed her harder, devouring all the sounds she made. Every thrust was faster and harder than the one before it, until he set a rhythm that was not about loving and exploring—it was about a release. One he needed in *her*. His growls echoed in the shower, and his fingers dug into her hip, pinning her where he needed her to stay. And he lost himself in all of her. Until she ripped her mouth away with a scream, her eyes wild with pleasure.

Yeah, he got why. He was hard. So fucking hard.

To have her—to truly have her—it was the dream he never knew he wanted until she came back into his life.

He held on tighter, thrust harder, and released all his frustrations, concerns, everything that was building inside him. And she let him. She held onto his neck and stared at him while he used her sweet body for his needs.

Until she tipped her chin back and fell into her orgasm, her hot, wet sex clenching at him. A minute later, he came in a wild rush with a loud growl and stumbled a little on the slippery floor before Alex got her other leg down quick. His muscles burned. His chest burned. Everything fucking burned.

"Well, that's one way to make yourself feel better," she eventually said with a soft laugh.

He slowly lifted his eyes and saw hers widen again with surprise. "Nothing about that was me trying to feel better." *I was making you mine.*

Obviously aware of his intention now, she said softly, "One step at a time, Rowan."

He'd already taken a big step forward; she just didn't

know it yet. Before he could say as much, she went on, "I know you're going through a lot, but it's time to get your head back in the game. I've found something."

"Which is?" he asked breathless.

She gave a slow-building smile. "I'm pretty sure I found our killer."

# CHAPTER 14

"TELL ME EVERYTHING again," Rowan said, as he held Alex's hand while they trotted down the staircase toward the lobby.

She'd never seen Rowan move so fast, but she knew right before she said, "I finally got into that server. It belongs to the FBI," that she was going to get a reaction. She just hadn't expected his reaction to be so intense. He moved swiftly to get dressed and ordered her to do the same. She grabbed jeans and a T-shirt from her bag that they'd brought back from the hotel. Within minutes, they were hurrying into the hallway. "There's nothing more to tell you than whoever used the dating app did so while at FBI headquarters," she reported, breathing deep from the exertion. "It'll take a lot more digging for me to find out who exactly the SiR profile belongs to in the FBI, but whoever it is, works there."

"Jesus fucking Christ," Rowan snapped. He stopped on the landing and turned to her, a vein protruding out of the middle of his forehead. "I kept wondering why I was getting the run-around. This is fucking why. It's someone on the inside."

"It also makes all this incredibly dangerous," she gently reminded him, considering he looked about a second away from storming into headquarters and demanding answers. "We're dealing with someone in the highest levels of law enforcement. Think of the access they have."

"I don't even want to consider that," Rowan said, letting out a long-frustrated breath. "And yet, it's one step closer to finding Mia."

She nodded, but also pointed out, "We need to get somewhere safe. All I know is if it were me, I would have safeguards on that server. He found us once before. He'll find us again, especially considering we know what we know."

Rowan's fingers tightened protectively around hers, and Alex felt the warmth swell in her chest. "And this time, he'll make sure we're eliminated for good."

The thought sent a chill right down to her bones. She nodded. "The game has changed now. We need to think this through from every angle."

"Yeah, we do." He pulled her in close, dropped a kiss on her forehead. "I've got somewhere safe that we can go."

Good. That was a start. Alex followed him down the stairs, and she stayed right on his heels as they entered the lobby. The bar was off to the right. The news was on the television screen they passed, and the reporter was discussing the last victim, Harriett Laurie, pretty face shown on the screen. Alex's stomach roiled with the thought that there was a very good chance this psychopath posed as one of the good guys. Even more so, she knew from her experience with Ryder that there was also a very good chance the killer was close to the case.

Rowan's friend Wes came to mind. She needed him checked out. Maybe it was time to bring Ryder into this.

Before Alex could pose that question, and just as they passed the security desk, Rowan suddenly stopped. She slowly turned to him, saw the concern on his face, and then everything happened fast from there.

A handful of men and women wearing FBI shirts and jackets and bulletproof vests closed in on them, weapons drawn. Rowan shoved her behind him, his gun trained out in front of him.

"Stand down," Wes yelled. "Hawke, stand down."

Alex felt her blood go ice cold. If it weren't for the handful of other FBI agents there, she'd grab Rowan, kiss him, knowing that would be her final goodbye. But she doubted Wes, if he were the killer, would take her out here.

Rowan's shoulders squared, and his voice lowered. "Not until you tell me what the fuck is going on here."

"She needs to come in," Wes said, cool and collected. "She hacked the server. And she has to answer for that."

Alex slowly turned to Rowan. His gaze was trained on Wes, burning fiercely with betrayal. She grabbed his arm, feeling the slight tremble of contained power. "Put your gun away. It's fine. I'll go in."

"Alex," Rowan warned, not taking his eyes off the targets around him.

She grabbed his hand and pushed it gently until he slowly lowered his weapon, and she turned to face him, keeping their conversation private. "Call Ryder. Look into Wes."

Confusion furrowed Rowan's brows for only a moment before clarity filled his expression. He grabbed her hand, tightening his fingers into hers. "I'll call a lawyer and get you out."

"Don't," she said. "Let me see where this goes."

Rowan pinched his lips shut tight, clearly restraining the string of curse words sitting on his tongue, and stayed rooted to the spot while Alex let Wes take her by the arm and lead her into the waiting black SUV.

The drive to the NYPD station was quick, as was getting her into an interrogation room. Metal table and chairs, a one-way mirror where she knew people were watching her from the other side. She kept her breath slow and steady, knowing one thing for certain: She was brought there to make a point. She simply needed to find out what that point was.

When the door finally opened, she expected Wes to

enter, but instead, she had to control the surprise engulfing her as the Director of the FBI, Carl Lewis, strode in. He was everything the FBI would want as their leader. Good-looking, in shape, held the classic all-American look with good teeth and neatly styled hair. "Hello, Ms. McCoy."

"Hello, Mr. Lewis." She clasped her hands tightly together under the table, confused by his arrival. Sure, he was doing the media rounds to keep the public at ease, but what did that have to do with her?

He took a seat at the table across from her, opening the button of his suit jacket as he sat. "I'm aware of your arrangement with both the FBI and the CIA. I also have no time to play games with you." He placed his hands flat against the table. "Why were you hacking into our databases today?"

"To be honest," she answered, releasing her hands to relax and kept her voice calm, "I hadn't known the server I was attempting to get into belonged to the FBI until I landed in the database." Which was actually the truth.

Lewis's gaze hardened. "You have not answered my question."

"I was paid by a wife to look into her husband who apparently has joined the dating app SiR," she lied breezily.

One eyebrow arched. "And that led to hacking into the FBI's databases?"

"Well, not exactly," she replied, with an easy shrug. "I discovered the husband belonged to the dating app SiR. After that, I fell down a rabbit hole there and eventually came across a server that wanted to keep me out. Of course, that intrigued me."

"And why is that?"

Again, she shrugged and was as honest as she could be. A lesson she learned from Ryder. Lying was easier when the truth was in there too. "It's like candy to a kid. Whenever I can't get in, I *want* to get in, but as I am sure you already know, the second I saw the server belonged to the FBI, I got out." She leaned forward a little, not letting this man shake her. She'd always been on the right side of the law, even if she had to go into the gray sometimes to catch the bad guys. "So, why exactly am I here, Mr. Lewis? You know who I am. You know what I do. You know I didn't do a damn thing when I hit that server." Which made her wonder what else he knew?

"You're here because what you did was illegal," he said. "I know you're working with Rowan Hawke to find his sister. Here is your official warning to back off. This is not his case, and any further interference will get you tossed in jail."

She sat back against her chair, folded her arms, and watched him a moment. She didn't have the knack to read people like Rowan could, but something about his warning rubbed her wrong. Going on that hunch, she offered, "What if I told you that I'm closing in on a suspect, and if I continue, I *will* find him?"

Lewis's jaw clenched. "I would tell you that you do not work for the FBI. Go home to San Francisco."

That answer made alarms go off her head. "Are you going to arrest me if I refuse to stop, then?" The thought was insane. And Rowan's frustration about being shut out now was totally understood, because the same damn thing was happening to her.

Why?

Again, his jaw clenched. He mirrored her posture by leaning back in his chair, folded his arms, and regarded her intently. "I brought you in today, Ms. McCoy, to remind you that while you have an obligation to your government, you do not have free rein. Again, this is your warning to back off and go home. There is no next time. Stop working this case immediately." He firmed his voice, squared his shoulders arrogantly. "Do I make myself perfectly clear?"

Oh, yeah, she got a whole lot, and right now, Wes was no longer looking guilty. "Perfectly."

He began to rise. "Go home, Ms. McCoy."

She followed his every move, and continuing on her hunch, she said, "Just so we're clear." He met her gaze again. "Your security is weak. The fact that I hit a server without knowing it means you have someone on the inside that is secretly using a server for their personal use.

They've weakened your system, and they've created a doorway into the FBI databases that I managed to break through. It's sloppy work, and had I had longer, I would have easily caught them. Let me know if you want that name, and"—she squared her shoulders arrogantly—"you should really get that fixed."

"We will take that under consideration." His eyes flared, and yet, there was something dead in his gaze that suddenly turned her blood to ice.

Something that felt oddly personal. Anger. Rage. Hatred. Directed at her.

The door opened, and Wes strode into the room, looking about as miserable as any man could look. She could only imagine that Rowan ripped him to shreds for allowing this to happen.

Lewis cupped Wes's shoulder on his way out the door. "Get her on a plane to San Francisco, and get back to work on the case. Balls to the wall to get this one put to bed."

"Yes, sir," Wes said.

And Alex, well, she just smiled, knowing she'd found their killer.

# CHAPTER 15

AN HOUR HAD passed since Alex was taken into custody. Rowan had placed the call to Ryder, only to find out from his office that Ryder was on a business trip to New York City. It didn't take long to realize that he'd come to help Alex, even though she adamantly refused him to join them. After that, Rowan had called and woken up a friend, who happened to be a lawyer, and was in the process of driving down to police headquarters, which was where Rowan waited now.

He paced in the alleyway across the street from headquarters, his fists clenching, while he did everything not to storm into that building and demand her release. The streetlights cut through the dark night, but the alleyway, stinking of garbage and God knows what else, kept Rowan hidden in the shadows.

"You broke your promise."

Rowan whirled around, catching sight of Ryder standing behind him before he also met his fist, sending Rowan's teeth chattering and his body flying back to hit the ground. Hard.

"You told me you would protect her," Ryder snarled, standing over him.

Rowan snorted, rubbed his jaw, easing the pain coursing through his face, then got onto his feet. "I don't have time for you." He went to turn away, focusing back on the headquarters' front doors, waiting for Alex to walk through them. But as he turned, he heard the click of a trigger. Slowly, he glanced back over his shoulder at Ryder. "You're fucking kidding me, right?"

Ryder's eyes narrowed to slits. His weapon remained trained on Rowan. "You've placed Alex into the hands of the FBI. Give me one very good reason why I shouldn't make you hurt a little for that?"

"Because you love me, and I really like him," Alex interjected.

Emotion rushed into Rowan as that *like* sure sounded awfully close to something much more real than that. He whirled around and didn't hesitate. He charged forward, had Alex in his arms in a split second, and laid the kiss on her he needed to have. She tensed, obviously in surprise, but then melted against him. "I called to get you released," he said after breaking the kiss.

"No, *I* called to get you released," Ryder stated firmly over Rowan's shoulder.

She rolled her eyes. "Well, I got myself released, so let's put the gun away, all right?" She gave Rowan a hard squeeze and a sweet smile. "Thank you for trying to get me out, though."

Rowan glanced her over. "You're all right?"

"Totally fine," she said, then she released him and moved closer to Ryder. She placed a hand on his arm, ignoring that Ryder continued to scowl at Rowan. "You are not supposed to be *here*. You could have sent me help without coming, and we both know that."

Ryder didn't even look at her, still snarling at Rowan. "I told you I did not like this. And this is why. He's putting you in danger."

"He's not putting me in any danger that I don't want to be in," she said. She seemed an expert at ignoring what he said, and instead continued, "It's sweet you came for me, thank you, but the last thing you need is to get yourself wrapped up in all this. You need to go home."

Ryder's gaze swept to her, tightened, and he examined her intently. "Tell me everything that happened."

That warning she gave sent off alarms in Rowan's head too. Her soft tone of voice. The worry in her eyes. It all raised the hairs on the back of Rowan's neck. He sidled up to her and took her hand, now feeling the slight tremble there. "Hold nothing back." On that front, he agreed with Ryder completely.

She paused then said with a voice holding a slight tremble too, "Our killer is Carl Lewis."

A beat.

"Are we talking about the Director of the FBI?" Ryder asked.

Alex nodded. "Yeah, *that* Carl Lewis."

Rowan processed this, taking it all in. Many times, killers liked placing themselves right in the middle of an investigation. It was why Alex suspected Wes, though Rowan had doubted that was the case, even though he'd planned to have Ryder look deeper, just in case his friendship with Wes made him wrong.

The more Rowan thought about it, the more he knew Lewis was right in the heart of this case, probably getting off on all the attention. Lewis being their killer also explained why everything seemed to be sitting at a standstill and why Rowan kept getting shut out. Though that realization sank heavy into his bones, because now he realized just how deep this ran in the FBI and how hard finding Mia would truly be.

Lewis was smart, educated, and high in power.

For his own peace of mind, Rowan slid his arm around Alex, bringing her closer as he asked, "What makes you so sure it's him?"

Alex glanced up, her gaze full of sympathy. "He said, 'balls to the wall.'"

Ryder snorted loudly. "I should have come sooner. How is that a way of identifying a killer?"

"It's a saying my sister told me once that the guy from SiR used often," Rowan explained before looking back at Alex. "Any chance you caught his tattoo too?"

"What tattoo?" Ryder asked.

Alex answered, "Mia told Rowan that the guy she'd been talking to had a big military tattoo on his back." She turned to Rowan and shook her head. "And, no, I didn't see it. He was wearing a jacket."

Ryder reached for his phone in his pocket. He texted as Alex continued, "But honestly, it's a feeling I got too." She turned to Rowan, those pretty eyes holding his intently. "He's just the type of man that you described, and when he spoke to me…"

"Wait," Rowan said, feeling the warmth leave his blood at that. "Lewis was there in headquarters today?"

"He was the one who interviewed me."

"That fucker," Rowan said, thrusting his fingers into his hair. Lewis had no reason to talk to Alex. Though the killer, knowing how close she was getting, would begin to unravel, make mistakes. "He gave you a warning, then, I take it?"

She gave a slow nod. "That's the way it felt to me. He told me to go home. He knows that we're digging. It sort of felt like he just wanted to make the point that he could get to me."

Rowan didn't like that. Not one fucking bit. And now, on top of his concern for Mia and his worry for his parents' emotional state, he knew he'd placed the woman who had worked her way into his cold heart in the direct line of fire.

Before he could say as much, Ryder asked, "Is this

the tattoo?"

Rowan turned toward Ryder's cell phone. The photograph was of a woman smiling on the beach in her bikini, but a man was in the background, his back facing the camera. The solider with a gas mask and a helicopter beneath it—it was all there. "Yeah, that's it. How did you get that?" Rowan asked.

"I told you before," Alex said. "Ryder has some good contacts."

Ryder cursed then shoved his phone back into his pockets. "Lewis is a good friend of a senator in New York City we provided protective detail for. They spent time together at the senator's lake house. One of the senator's daughters had caught Lewis in that photograph. I had to request she take it down off social media, but of course, we kept the photograph on our server." He straightened his shoulders and then frowned at Rowan. "You know what you've done, then, don't you?"

Alex glanced between them. "What have you done?" she finally asked Rowan.

Of course Rowan knew, even without the judgmental gaze of Ryder glaring him down. He had known it a second ago. "I've made the woman I care very much about the target of a very powerful and brutal serial killer."

"Well…" Alex said, focusing entirely on Rowan, "it's a damn good thing that this woman is the one woman who can take him down and find Mia."

He expected Alex's strength, though now everything had changed. He cupped her face. "I can't ask you to be a part of this anymore. Not with Lewis involved. It's too dangerous, and he now knows you're driving this show."

She leaned into his touch, and her eyes warmed. And suddenly Rowan felt like he wasn't the only one who realized this time things had changed between them. This time, it wouldn't be so easy to walk away when all was said and done.

Maybe this time they would both choose to stay.

"You don't have to ask me, Rowan," she said, breaking the silence. "I'm in this. Until the end. Until we find Mia."

"I'm with Rowan," Ryder added. "This is too dangerous now. You're out of this. I'll bring in another hacker."

She glanced between them and snorted. "So, now you're suddenly getting along?" She placed her hands on her hips and glared at them. "I've had more than enough of arrogant men than I can stomach tonight. I'm going to find Mia, with or without the help from either of you." She turned and headed down the alleyway, the dark night swallowing her.

Rowan slowly glanced at Ryder. "Is she always like this?"

"She's usually worse." He grinned before following Alex.

Rowan smiled too. Damn, she was perfect.

READ ON FOR A SNEAK PEEK AT THE
CONCLUSION OF THE *DIRTY HACKER* SERIES:

## RISKY LOVE

*USA Today bestselling author Stacey Kennedy is back with
the thrilling and emotional conclusion of the Dirty Hacker
duet about a hacker who doesn't back down on a case, a sexy
CIA agent who is more than a little overprotective, and two
slightly reluctant but perfectly matched hearts.*

Tracking a killer is the last thing hacker Alex McCoy
expected out of her vacation to New York, but after
rekindling her one-time romance with sexy CIA Agent
Rowan Hawke, she can't refuse his request for help.
Waiting for a break in the case proves to be more
challenging than Alex expected, especially because it gives
her too much time to think about her growing feelings
for Rowan. Feelings she would much rather write off as

the intensely hot chemistry between them.

Rowan knows that Alex has a lot of emotional baggage, but every day as they work together, he becomes more certain she's the woman for him. Unfortunately, Rowan's instinct to protect her is put to the test when secrets come to light and Alex throws herself in the line of fire to help Rowan solve the case. As Rowan falls deeper for Alex, he must open up about his past and give her the chance to prove that she's the right partner—in work and in life.

Alex and Rowan are up against a powerful perpetrator, with only their courage and their love for each other to help them through. But Alex's choice to run head-first into danger might be the one thing that breaks them apart…permanently.

Find out more about *Risky Love*.
Stay up-to-date with Stacey's new releases and join the mailing list HERE.
staceykennedy.com/newsletter

# CHAPTER 1

"THAT DIRTY, FUCKING psychopath," Alex McCoy grumbled beneath her breath as FBI Director, Carl Lewis, exited NYPD police headquarters. The street was bustling with cars and congestion, horns blaring through the dark night, while Alex sat in the driver's seat of her rented SUV. Lewis strode with purpose toward the limo waiting at the curb, with all the arrogance and entitlement that he'd been handed. In the public's eye, Lewis was the face of the investigation of New York City's latest serial killer whom the media had coined the Casanova Sadist. Only thing: Carl Lewis *was* the Casanova Sadist—the man responsible for killing six women he'd stalked on the BDSM dating app SiR for his sadistic games. Typically, the app was used by sane people looking to keep their kinky interludes private, but it also gave Lewis the perfect hunting ground. Two more women were still missing. And the FBI had no suspects, no DNA evidence...*nothing.*

The dark night had crept on Alex at some point while she'd waited for Lewis to exit the police station.

On the outside, Lewis was like any other businessman in a suit. His dark hair was styled with gel. His round face clean-shaven. His suit, crisp and clean, and fitting him perfectly. On the inside, Lewis was a disgusting human that needed to be put down. And as the best hacker in North America, Alex was going to catch him.

"That *dangerous*, dirty, fucking psychopath, you mean," the low, seductive voice said through her earpiece. The voice belonged to CIA agent Rowan Hawke, her one-time lover in Paris five years ago while they'd worked a case together, turned again lover these past days they'd been working the Casanova Sadist case, and the man who would officially end Lewis. Lewis's latest abduction victim was Rowan's younger sister, Mia.

A major error in judgment on Lewis's part.

Rowan would never stop looking for his sister until she was home and safe.

As Lewis climbed into the limo, Alex turned on the ignition of her rented silver Honda Civic. "It's been two days of following this prick. When is he going to fuck up?"

"We have to consider we might be wrong," Rowan said, his voice tight through the earpiece.

Alex pondered that as she pulled out in traffic a few cars back from the limo. They were getting nowhere fast, but she still trusted her instincts. Lewis exposed himself as the Casanova Sadist all because of his own ego. He'd been in control of this case from the inside. When he tried to exert that control over Alex, bringing her in to interrogate her about why she worked a case that didn't have approval from both the CIA and the FBI, he said the words *balls to the wall* and tipped himself off as the killer. He meant it as a way to get a fire burning under his team, but Mia had told Rowan that the new man in her life she texted often said the line.

While it was an odd identifier, the saying was unusual enough that Alex knew they had their guy. Instincts most times didn't make sense. But her instincts all pointed in Lewis's direction. Particularly because Mia had also mentioned her new guy had a large military tattoo on his back of a soldier with a gas mask and a helicopter beneath it, which Lewis had too.

"He's our guy," she said, glancing at Rowan out the passenger side window as she drove by while he sat on his sleek silver motorcycle. He wore all black, which included a black helmet. Rowan was all muscle, all man, and for the past few days, he was all hers. And she happened to like that. Even now, at the worst time possible, just the sight of Rowan made her skin flush. His helmet turned, following her direction while she drove by as she went on. "I've got no doubt in my mind."

"And you've got my trust," Rowan replied.

Alex felt the warmth of his words touch her chest. She quickly refocused on following the limo. They had enough going on without diving into a conversation they should have had five years ago. The one that would put two people who didn't do relationships firmly into one. Five years ago, they'd both run to avoid that question.

But that was then. And even Alex felt the shift in her that indicated maybe this time she wouldn't run when it came time to talking about their future.

Soon, they eased out of Manhattan traffic and into Brooklyn's busy streets, until the roads cleared and they were heading into a swankier area with mansions sitting atop manicured gardens with flowerbeds and plant art for as far as the eye could see. Alex wasn't exactly sure where Rowan was, never heard the hum of his motorcycle behind her, but he'd stay close. She trusted him too.

"Do you know where he's going?" Alex asked.

"Give me a few on that," Ryder Blackwood said through the earpiece, having kept quiet so far, as this was not his show. Ryder owned Blackwood Security back in San Francisco, and he was also Alex's boss. When he retired from the Army Rangers, Ryder had formed a security company, hiring many of his military buddies. There was no one better when it came to tactical security, something the government knew and contracted him for.

A big part of Alex didn't want Ryder anywhere near this. Not with this killer now aware they were coming after him, and certainly not when Ryder had a wife and new baby son at home. But Ryder was careful and cautious, and she knew without a doubt he'd taken all precautions and that he likely appeared to the FBI as if he were working another case entirely. She trusted him as a boss, she loved him like a brother.

She followed the limo down another street to the right and then spotted Lewis's limo driving up to a gated house. Alex caught the number before driving by. "The house number is 1002."

"Yeah, we see that," Ryder said. He was working out of his New York City headquarters, set up with his command center back in San Francisco, no doubt following Lewis with satellite imagery the government gave Ryder full access to.

"I'm taking up location on the east side of the property," Rowan said.

Only then did Alex see Rowan on his bike whizz by her and turn left, vanishing from sight. She pulled over behind a construction company truck, hoping that kept her out of view. Just as she cut the ignition, she spotted the gate opening again. "Limo's leaving. No idea if Lewis is in it. Do I follow?" she asked.

"Stay put," Rowan said. "I want to know why he came here and whose house this is."

Ryder's team in New York City had already investigated Lewis's condo in Manhattan. They didn't discover anything, which included not finding a personal computer. Alex needed to get her hands on his PC.

"It's his great aunt's house," Ryder finally answered. "She's been dead a year."

Alex glanced back at the gates and scanned the area, reassessing. The mansions had to have price tags upwards of ten million dollars. "Does he spend time here?"

"Checking on that," Ryder said. The limo had vanished down the road when Ryder reported, "Not that we can see. He seems to split time between Washington and New York City, but he's got an apartment here that he uses, not this house."

A beat passed. Hope silently passed through the air between them all, as this was the first location Lewis had been to where he didn't have a good reason for being there. Add that to the fact that his holding onto the property made no sense.

Rowan broke the silence. "We need to get into that house."

"I'm coming to you now," Ryder said. "Don't make a move without me."

Unsure if Rowan would follow that order, Alex turned on the car and made her way over to the east side of the property. She quickly spotted Rowan sitting on his bike parked on the side of the road, one boot on the curb. On this side of the street, there were no gated entryways or streetlights. She parked behind him and grabbed her backpack of supplies, then exited the car.

His shoulders were tense and rigid when she approached. Before she said a word, she clicked off her earpiece and waited for Rowan to remove his helmet to do the same. "Ryder won't be long," she told him.

Those steely gray eyes met hers. Urgency sparked between them, as he nodded, no doubt torn between wanting to do the smart thing and have backup, and rushing in to find his sister. Rowan put out the kickstand and hopped off his bike, leaving his helmet on the gas tank. He moved to the small compartment area beneath the seat and took out his gun, loading it with bullets then offering it to her.

"Ah, yeah, so that's your and Ryder's job," she said, taking a step back.

Rowan caught her hand. "We don't know what we're walking into." He placed the gun in her hand. "Don't hesitate."

She wrapped her fingers around the cool metal.

Rowan gave a firm nod of approval.

By the time he got himself armed to the teeth, Ryder arrived, pulling in behind Rowan in his rented truck. Ryder strode toward them and offered them both bulletproof vests. "Safety first."

"Thanks." Alex quickly got into hers.

"You clear upstairs," Rowan said to Ryder, fastening his vest. To Alex, he added, "We'll clear the basement and work our way up."

Alex restrained her smile at Ryder's small frown. He'd want her with him, she didn't doubt that, but he must have trusted Rowan slightly since he finally nodded. "Be aware of odd placements of rugs, cracks in walls. Lewis may have a room that's not visible."

"Can you do a thermal scan on the property?" Alex asked.

Ryder's mouth twitched. "The team's already on it."

"Thank you," Rowan said, then looked at Alex, his lips thinning. "Stay close."

She gave a quick nod, holding her gun how Ryder had taught her, down and out, ready to act if needed. It surprised her that Rowan let Ryder lead the way, but then she realized by Rowan's closeness right in front of her, there was a very good reason for that.

*Her.*

He kept his body like a shield in front of her, seemingly aware of her behind him, as he trudged into the forest and she followed, her eyes quickly adjusting to the dark night. The moon was bright, both illuminating their path but also letting their whereabouts be known. When the looming house appeared, there wasn't a light on or any sign indicating Lewis was still in the house. The mansion stood like a dark shadow, and a sliver of hope ran up her spine. This place provided the exact location Lewis needed.

Ryder reached the house first and quickly picked the

lock of the basement's door. In seconds, they were inside. The basement was an open space full of boxes. Rowan clicked a flashlight on, and Alex followed as quietly as she could. Barely breathing, walking lightly on her feet, she stayed behind Rowan as he moved through the basement with lethal precision. When Rowan went right, Alex went left, glancing over the floor as she went, looking for any sign of a trap door. She then studied the walls, but only found concrete.

When she reached the stairs to the upper floor, Rowan met her there. "It's clear that way," she told him.

He nodded. "Let's go up."

They quietly traveled up the stairs that Ryder must have gone up too. The door was left ajar, and they made it onto the main level. Rowan cleared the kitchen, and Alex searched the living room and sitting room, finding nothing out of the ordinary, except clean furniture. And that in itself still rubbed her wrong. Why put such care into a property he didn't use?

Alex ended up in the library, where she spotted the computer on the grand desk. She moved there immediately and grabbed a portable hard drive from her backpack. She plugged it in and powered up the computer, and it booted up to the cloning utility. In the minutes it took her to clone Lewis's computer, Rowan had strode into the room, looking frustrated but at ease, with Ryder following.

"Nothing?" Alex asked softly.

Rowan shook his head. "Lewis isn't here, and neither is my sister." He gestured at the computer. "Got anything there?"

"Just cloning the files." When the application stopped running, she took out the portable hard drive. "I don't know if this actually belongs to Lewis, but if it does, I'll have work to do to get into his secured files. He'd be smart about his security." She rose. "Come on, let's get out of here."

Right as she took a step, Rowan held up a hand, then reached for his phone that had obviously vibrated as it rang. He had it to his ear in the next second. "Hawke." A long pause followed as Rowan's expression went totally closed. "I'm coming now." He shut his eyes, and the phone was still pressed to his ear, even though Alex suspected the call had ended.

The space between them suddenly felt cold. She needed to get closer, and hurried to his side, reaching for his hand, clutching his trembling fingers. "What's happened?"

"That was Wes"—his buddy that worked for the FBI and had been working the Casanova Sadist case—"they found Mia."

Ryder took a step closer.

"God, Rowan, I'm so sorry," Alex barely managed. She understood all too well how it felt to lose a sister.

She lost hers when she was seventeen. Her chest hollowed at the darkness around him. She recognized that pain, and she wanted to drain it from him, squeezing his hand tighter, hoping he knew she was in this with him. They'd fought through all this together, and his pain now felt like hers too. "I'm just so damn sorry we didn't get there in time."

He finally opened his eyes, and she sucked in a harsh breath at the raw emotion flaring there as he said, "They found her alive."

# About the Author

Stacey Kennedy is an outdoorsy, wine-drinking, nap-loving, animal-cuddling, USA Today bestselling romance author with a chocolate problem. She writes sexy contemporary romance full of heat and heart, including titles in her wildly hot Dangerous Love, Kinky Spurs, Dirty Little Secrets and Club Sin series. She lives in southwestern Ontario with her family and does most of her writing surrounded by lazy dogs.

Learn more at:
www.staceykennedy.com
Twitter @Stacey_Kennedy
Facebook.com/authorstaceykennedy

Get a FREE book by subscribing to Stacey's newsletter:
www.staceykennedy.com/newsletter

# Acknowledgments

To my husband, my children, family, friends, and bestie, it's easy to write about love when there is so much love around me. Big thanks to my readers for your friendship and your support; my editor, Christa, for believing in me and making my stories shine; my agent, Jessica, for always having my back; the kick-ass authors in my sprint group for their endless advice and support. Thank you.